CW01649913

'How a [illegible]
Lucille c[illegible] believe her ears. They were in darkness, but now it was as if a great light had dawned.
'Say that again!' she whispered, trembling.
'Say what?' he teased, and then once more he took her in his arms. But this time there was passion, not comfort, in his clasp. As he bent to kiss her and their lips met, they forgot their danger, forgot they still had a long hard way ahead of them.
It wasn't the right time or the right place, but when love comes, there is never time, nor place, only eternity!

Also by Daisy Thomson in *Star*

WOMAN IN LOVE
SUMMONS TO LOVE
JOURNEY TO LOVE
PORTRAIT OF MY LOVE
PRELUDE TO LOVE
TO LOVE AND HONOUR
BE MY LOVE

Daisy Thomson

A TRUCE FOR LOVE

A STAR BOOK
published by
the Paperback Division of
W. H. ALLEN & Co. Ltd.

A Star Book
Published in 1977
by the Paperback Division of
W. H. Allen & Co. Ltd
a Howard and Wyndham Company
44 Hill Street, London W1X 8LB

First published in Great Britain by
Robert Hale Ltd, 1967
Copyright © D. H. Thomson 1967

Printed in Great Britain by
Cox & Wyman Ltd, London, Reading and Fakenham

ISBN 0 352 39545 1

This book is sold subject to the condition that it shall not, by way of trade or otherwise, be lent, re-sold, hired out or otherwise circulated without the publisher's prior consent in any form of binding or cover other than that in which it is published, and without a similar condition including this condition being imposed on the subsequent purchaser

CHAPTER ONE

I stopped for lunch at the Hotel in Castellane where I have stopped for the past five years on my journey to Tourloup les Alpes.

The head waiter, with that amazing memory for faces which good head waiters seem to possess, came forward, smiling, to meet me.

'Ah! Mademoiselle! You are back again!' He gave his courteous little bow before leading me to the best table in the dining-room, a table for two in the window alcove which overlooked the geranium filled garden.

'I trust, Mademoiselle, that for you the weather will improve,' he continued, as he pulled out the chair for me. 'Here as in all France, the winter and spring have been cold and wet, and only now the sun begins to shine.'

He beckoned one of his underlings to bring me a menu card and hovered discreetly in the background, listening to my choice of dishes and nodding approvingly as I selected those items for which the chef was noted, and which I remembered with enjoyment from previous visits.

After the meal, I asked the waiter to convey my appreciation to the kitchen, and then I went to the powder room to have a wash and replace my travel-wilted woollen shirt with a crisp, white blouse. Then I combed my honey brown hair smoothly back from my forehead, slipped on a broad white bandeau to keep it neatly in place, creamed my cheeks and tip-tilted nose against the burning of the sun which was magnified by the windscreen of my Rapier, added a touch of red to my lips, and feeling inwardly and outwardly refreshed I set out on the last stage of my journey.

When, a few miles later on, I turned off the busy N.85 on to the narrow, grit covered road which serpents its way up through the Alpes Maritimes to Tourloup, my veins tingled with the excited anticipation I always feel when I arrive at what I think of as the 'home' stretch.

Since my parents were killed in an air crash four years ago and I had to sell the family house and store those belongings with which I did not want to part, I have lived in a small service flat in Edinburgh, which I share with a fellow student, but this flat could hardly be thought of in terms of a home. For me it was merely a place to eat and sleep and study until I graduated, and decided what I wanted to do and where I intended to settle down, once I was Lucille Mathieson, M.A.

The Lucille part of my name is for my French grandmother, for my mother had come from Tourloup, and I was on my way back there to the one place I could still think of as home, for my grandfather, Jean Pierre Verlaine, still lived and worked there, and welcomed me with warmth and love each summer of my life.

I smiled to myself as I thought of him. He was not at all the cartoonist's image of the average Frenchman.

He was a great, tall, barrel of a man, with enormous hands, the strength of a Clydesdale, a rumbustious sense of humour and a great deep bellow of a laugh which someone once remarked could be heard from one end of Tourloup to the other. In fact, he looked more like the jolly 'mine host' of an English hostelry than the clever lawyer and notary public of a small French commune.

His house, kept spick and span for him since his wife's death by an excellent housekeeper, was tall and narrow and overlooked the great gorge which effectively cut Tourloup off from access from the south. The rooms were cool and shady in summer, and, because Martha loved plants, almost overflowing with trailing greenery of ivies, rubber plants and vines. The window sills were decorated with boxes filled with geraniums and salvias and petunias, but the heart of the place, where we dined unless there was company, was the kitchen with its polished range, its gleaming brass pots and pans, and its indescribable aroma of onions and over-ripe brie, and new baked bread, and herbs—

In spite of my recent lunch, my salivary glands began to flow at the thought of tasting again the dishes which Martha prepared with the expertise which would have won her a cordon bleu at Atholl Cresent, or a star rating with Micheline.

As I reached the Col de Lune, the second highest point of the road before it dipped to rise again for the final climb to Tourloup, a glance at my watch told me that if I proceeded at my usual pace I would arrive at my destination an hour before I was expected, and this would never do. Grandpère would not be home from the office and if I arrived before he did, Martha would get into a flap – and when Martha flapped, she flapped!

For her sake, as well as for Grandpère's and my own, I decided to dally for an hour before arriving at Tourloup.

I remembered a convenient parking place a mile further on, and here I turned off the road and stopped in the shelter of a pine wood, near a trail which led down to the river.

I left the car windows open so that it would keep relatively cool, took the key from the ignition and put it in my shoulder bag, and strolled off down the pine-needle covered pathway until I came to a big water meadow.

I kicked off my shoes and sat on a smooth boulder by the water's edge, dipping my toes into water which was clear as the finest crystal and ice-cold from the snows which brought the stream into being high up among the crags of the Mont de la Lune.

The sun was warm as a blessing and the air soft as the touch of satin on my skin and perfumed with the resin of the pine trees and the rosemary and myrtle which grew on the far hillside.

I lay back and looked up at the lowering mountain on my right. It was because of this great peak, with its head eternally white with snow, that my parents had met.

My father's plane, hit by flak after a raid on Milan in the Second World War, had failed to clear the Alp. Three of the crew had successfully bailed out. Two were captured by German patrols, but my father, the third survivor, had been caught by an air current and in his parachute blown over the Lune gorge, so that he had come down within sight of the village of Tourloup.

Two days later he had been found with a broken ankle, and weak with exposure, by members of the local Resistance group, hidden by them, and in particular by Jean Pierre Verlaine, nursed back to health by my mother, and later guided to the escape route to Switzerland by another underground worker.

In September 1945, he returned to Tourloup to ask Marguerite Verlaine to be his bride and, with the blessing of the local people, he married her and brought her to his home in Scotland.

Every summer Angus Mathieson and his wife returned to Tourloup and I would be only months old when I paid my first visit there. I grew to know and love the village and its people as well as I did my own home town of Inchtain. Perhaps this was because I found a strong similarity between the individualistic people of this once Huguenot stronghold akin to the people of my own Scottish background, and it could have been this similarity of spirit and character which had made my father acceptable to Jean Pierre Verlaine as a husband for his only child.

The people of Tourloup were proud, canny and courageous, as their record during the years of resistance showed, but though courteous to strangers, they did not give their friendship easily. Yet my father had been liked and welcomed by all of them from the rather pompous Mayor, Didenot, to the gentle goatherd, Jules Lamartine, who before the war had been an up-and-coming portrait painter but who had never held a brush again after the Germans had crushed and mutilated his hands because of his suspected resistance activities.

It was Jules who had told me more of the history and topography of Tourloup than either of my parents. Jules who had shown me the best pools to fish in the river Lune; the places where the finest mushrooms grew to gather for Martha's omelettes and stews. Jules who, on oath of secrecy,

Without taking time to wipe them clean, or even to brush the sharp, brown pine-needles from my skirt, I got into the car, slammed the door shut, started the engine and, sending out a spray of moss and loose earth from the back spin of the wheels, I shot out on to the roadway and raced towards Tourloup.

CHAPTER TWO

I was in such a hurry to get to my grandfather and tell him of my unhappy find, that I did not take the precautions I usually take on this notoriously twisty section of the road to Tourloup. The sharp corners are all blind and it is advisable to sound one's horn long and loud when approaching the bends.

Today, however, I forgot all about this safety measure and, as I came rocketing round one particularly fierce hair-pin, it was only by the grace of God that I escaped being killed. Had the reflexes of either the oncoming driver or myself been even a fraction of a second slower, we would have met head on with appalling results, but as it was, in that instant of time before what seemed an inevitable crash, we both automatically swung our wheels round and acceler-ated, thereby missing each other by little more than a razor blade's breadth.

The Alfa's driver was, however, more fortunate even than I. There was a rough embankment of grit and scree some ten feet wide on his side of the road, before it dropped sheerly down into the gorge, and this gave him a comfortable safety margin.

I, on the other hand, was on the side of the road which had been cut out of a great cliff face, and only about a couple of feet of rubble stood between the verge of the road and the mountain wall.

Biting my lip in my anxiety, the moment the collision with

the oncoming car had been averted, I hastily pulled the wheel round again to bring me back on to the road, and for a moment I thought I was going to emerge scatheless from the adventure. Unfortunately, there was an outcrop of limestone projecting from the cliff face about a foot above the ground. It caught the edge of my headlamp with a sickening crunch and scraped raspingly along the wing as I pulled clear.

Since I was far enough from the corner not to cause an obstruction and still partly off the road, I braked to a stop and got out to examine the damage.

It actually was not as bad as the noise of the impact had made me believe, but the headlamp glass was splintered and there was a disfiguring scrape mark along the pale blue paintwork of the right wing. As I stood staring at the mark in disgust, hurrying footsteps from the road behind me made me look round. A tallish man, with black hair and a deeply sun-tanned face, was coming towards me, and I had no doubts, as the driver of the Italian car, he would be very voluble and excited.

The fright I had had, had made me angry. After all, I told myself, I hadn't been entirely to blame for what had happened. True, I had been driving a shade fast for the road conditions and I hadn't taken the precaution of sounding my horn before I rounded the corner, but the same went for this man too.

I opened my mouth to tell him exactly what I thought of his driving abilities, but he got in the first words.

'You stupid woman!' he raged in English, in a voice whose angry tone failed to hide unexpected Highland softness. 'Surely even the greenest G.B. driver knows better than to act like a speed demon on a road like this!'

'It's you who obviously doesn't know the rule of the road in this part of the country!' I flared back. 'Down-coming traffic always has to give way to up-coming traffic on an Alpine road. And what's more,' I went on before he could interrupt, 'not only were you racing downhill far too quickly, but you didn't even blow your horn!'

'You didn't sound yours either,' he snapped back. 'And,' he glared at me, 'you cut the corner!'

'Nonsense!' I retorted, and my green eyes glared up into his hazel ones. 'You simply do not have the grace to admit you were in the wrong and because I am a woman, you are trying to brow-beat me into thinking I made the mistake.'

He opened his mouth to reply, but I went on, acid in every tone, 'If you had been Italian, as I had deduced you were from the car, you would have courteously conceded your liability.'

'For heaven's sake!' He shook his head. 'You were in the wrong,' he said categorically. 'But I'll bet you were hoping that by striking up a damsel-in-distress attitude and fluttering your eyelashes at some poor male with a weakness for pretty blondes, you would get away with it! Well, let me tell you—'

'You will tell me nothing!' I gritted at him. 'We'll keep personalities out and do as the law requires. If you give me your name and address, so that I can give them to my insurance bureau – and there's a "huissier" in Touloup who will give us a "procès verbal" and—'

'My! My!' interrupted the man, with a mocking lift of his thick, dark eyebrows. 'You sound as if you had been in trouble before for your driving in France, the way all the technical terms come dripping off your tongue!'

'I have never had any driving accidents, either here or home in Britain,' I said coldly. 'I merely like to know something about the laws of the country in which I happen to be. So, now, if I can have your name and address?'

'Skip it!' said the man wearily. 'My car hasn't been damaged and I have no bones broken, so there is no need for us to get bogged down by useless legal formalities.'

'Then why did you stop and come back here?' I wanted to know.

'I had to make sure nothing had happened to you. However stupid they are, I feel it is my duty to help fellow countrymen.'

'How very noble of you!' I said sarcastically.

He ignored the sarcasm. 'Since you seem to be unhurt, I shall get on my way. I am in a hurry.'

'You don't need to tell me that!' I put in hastily.

He ignored me and went on, 'I am supposed to be at the Cote D'Azur airport at seven o'clock, so I am cutting it rather fine. That is why any kind of formalities would hinder me, so,' he took out a wallet from his pocket, extracted a card, scribbled something on it and proffered it to me.

'Here you have my name and address. To save any argument, have the bill for the damage to your car sent to me.'

'If your car isn't damaged, let's forget the whole thing, shall we?' I replied. 'The garage in Tourloup will put my wing right for me for next to nothing.'

'That sounds very un-French of them,' he remarked. 'Or is it that the mechanic there has let himself be taken in by your wide-eyed charm?'

'Oh!' I gasped indignantly. Never in my life had I come across such a rude, insufferable male and I saw no reason to explain to him that Jacques, the mechanic and now part owner of Tourloup's one garage, was an old friend of mine. That, in fact, we had known each other since childhood when we had shared many a crusty loaf and slab of chocolate Meunier while catching tadpoles in the water meadows of the Lune.

'Oh!' I reiterated, taking the card he had given me and angrily ripping it to pieces without even glancing at his name. 'I hope I never, never come across you again!'

So saying, I flounced back into my car, noisily revved the engine and let off the handbrake.

'Remember and sound your horn at the next corner,' the maddening man called derisively after me as I moved off. 'I shall be seeing you!'

Oh no, you won't, my lad, I thought grimly, and anger at the impertinence of the dark visaged Scot, with his mocking eyes, so filled my mind that it was not until I was bumping over the cobbles of Tourloup High Street, that I thought once more about the body which indirectly had been responsible for my near accident.

A look at the clock on the town hall told me Grandfather would still be in his office. He was most meticulous about his time-keeping. Even knowing I was coming today, would not make him depart from his routine. There was even a joke in the village about this. People said you could set your watches as accurately by the movements of Jean Verlaine as you could by the radio time signal.

The motor car has not yet taken over the streets of Tourloup and, except in the height of the summer season, when visitors come to see the gorge of Lune, the ruins of the Chateau de Mercredi, and the very beautiful monument erected to the Resistance fighters on the spot where they were massacred, there are rarely more than half a dozen cars to be seen, so I was able to find a parking place right outside the office.

Grandpère looked up in surprise as I came hurrying into his private chamber. My arrival at this time was so contrary to custom that he immediately suspected something must be wrong.

'Lucille!' he came forward and kissed me warmly on both cheeks. 'Lucille, ma chérie? Qu'est ce qu'il y a?'

At the concern in his voice, something inside me seemed to snap. The excitement which had kept me going from the moment of discovery at the river, through the strain of my near fatal crash and my argument with the other driver involved, evaporated.

I clung to my grandfather, my whole body trembling.

He held me close to him, patting my back and uttering soothing words of comfort.

'There, there, ma petite,' he said gently. 'Tell me all about it.'

Gradually my fit of the shivers passed and I pulled myself from his arms.

'I'm sorry about that,' I smiled weakly. 'I suppose it was reaction, but I'm all right now.'

'Then sit over here, Lucille,' he led me to the big leather chair with the poker-stiff back facing the window, which he reserved for his clients.

'Now, when you have composed yourself, tell me all about it.' He gave me a shrewd look. 'You haven't knocked someone down with that car of yours?'

I flushed, thinking of my narrow recent escape, but shook my head.

'It has nothing to do with my driving,' I told him. 'It's just – Grandfather,' I looked directly at him, 'half an hour or so ago, I found a body in the river below the Col de la Lune!'

My grandfather isn't often shaken, but my statement certainly made him start.

'Lucille! What is this you say?'

'It was like this, Grandpapa,' I began slowly, my hands fidgeting nervously with the hem of my skirt. 'I had made very good time for Grenoble—'

'You drive too fast!' my grandfather interrupted. 'You worry me. One day – but never mind – you were saying.'

'I arrived at Castellane for an early lunch, the roads were clear,' I grimaced at him, 'and I found myself at the Col de la Lune a good hour before I meant to arrive here.'

'Yes?'

'Grandpapa, you know what Martha is like! If I had arrived at the Villa Beau Site before she was expecting me, she would have been so upset – and I knew better,' I teased him, 'than to interrupt you here in normal circumstances. So, I decided I would have a peaceful hour down by the river enjoying the sun, until it was near enough to the time I was expected here.'

'So?' My grandfather's eyes never left my face.

'Well, I parked the car off the road, under the pines, and wandered down the bank to a little water meadow and sat for a while half dozing in the sun.'

I took a deep breath.

'It was when I was about to leave that I saw what I took to be a bundle of rags caught up by a branch at the water's edge.' I closed my eyes, feeling a return of nausea, but willed myself to go on.

'I was curious, so I prodded it with a stick. The prodding

set it free. It rolled over and,' I looked at my grandfather, 'It wasn't a bundle of rags at all. It was a man's body!'

Grandfather sucked in a startled breath.

'You are quite sure of that, Lucille?'

'Of course I am!' I said indignantly.

'Then we had better get to the police right away and report this! They will want to recover it as soon as possible.'

I bit my lip.

'That's the difficulty, Grandfather,' I explained. 'The body is no longer where I found it. When it drifted free from the branch, the current caught it – and you know what the current of the Lune is like when there has been a lot of rain – it could be anywhere by this time.'

Grandfather pursed his lips.

'What a pity you had to poke away at it!'

'If I hadn't, I wouldn't have known it *was* a body!' I protested indignantly.

'I suppose there's that to it,' he nodded. 'And now, we have to go and tell Sergeant Duval about it.' He went to get his hat from the rack.

'I suppose so,' I said drearily.

Grandfather gave me a sympathetic look.

'I know it has been a horrible experience for you, my child, and you do not want to talk about it, but one has to do one's duty, so the sooner you give Duval all the details, the sooner you will be able to forget about it.'

He put on his hat.

'By the way,' he added, as an afterthought, 'I take it you did not recognize the body, or you would have said so.'

'No,' I replied truthfully. After all, why mention that I thought I had seen the face before, when I could recall neither the time nor the place, and when, indeed, the look of familiarity might have only been imagined. Such information would be of no help to the police.

'Alors!' said Grandfather briskly. 'To Sergeant Duval!'

He glanced at his watch. 'But first, I think I had better telephone our good Martha and explain that you are with me, and that we shall be home a little later than expected.'

While he telephoned the housekeeper, I took the opportunity to try and tidy myself. There were still pine-needles from the embankment sticking into my skirt, and the dust had dried into my hands.

Not only that, I realized with annoyance as I glanced at a mirror – there was a great, dirty smear across my forehead where I had pushed my hair back from my eyes after my hurried scramble up the bank, and the crisp blouse I had changed into in Castellane was limp and grubby.

This must have been the untidy picture I had presented to the objectionable driver of the Alfa Romeo, and I flushed with anger as I recalled how he had sneered about my making use of my feminine charm! He had actually been mocking me more than I had appreciated at the time!

Oh! If I ever saw him again, I would tell him a thing or two, I decided wrathfully, as I washed my hands and face in the toilet behind Grandfather's office, and hastily applied lipstick and powder, more as a morale booster than for beautification!

I returned to the office, hoping Grandfather would not be impatient at being kept waiting.

To my surprise, he was no longer alone.

Standing talking to him, looking handsomer, more debonair and much more sophisticated than ever, was Raoul Médoc, the journalist son of the local doctor, and the man who, two summers ago, had asked me to marry him.

CHAPTER THREE

Raoul looked at me with a welcoming smile as I came into the room.

'Lucille!' He came forward, hands outstretched, to greet me. 'Lucille,' he shook my hand. 'It is good to see you again!'

His dark blue eyes looked directly into mine and he gripped my hand much longer than convention demanded.

I flushed at the intensity of his gaze. 'Raoul! It is good to see you, too! And a surprise! Grandpapa did not tell me you were home again.' Gently I pulled my hand from his restraining grip.

'Much time I've had to tell you any local news!' snorted Grandfather. 'You have been doing all the talking since you arrived.'

I looked up at Raoul.

'Has Grandpère told you what happened to me?'

He nodded, a teasing smile on his lips.

'He did, Lucille, but I'm afraid,' the smile broadened, 'I refuse to take your story seriously. A dead body in our river, indeed!'

'But it's true!' I cried indignantly. 'If you don't believe me, I shall take you to the very spot where I found it!'

'But there is no body there now, is there?' he demanded, still grinning. 'I understand it floated conveniently away!'

'There was a body!' I protested. 'In dark clothes and—'

'Chère Lucille,' Raoul interrupted, 'I'll believe in the bundle of clothes, but a body – bah! It's that vivid imagination of yours. You see some rags and imagine a corpse! It reminds me of those fantastic tales you used to tell me as a child.' He shook his head. 'It was always difficult to know when reality stopped and fantasy took over,' he teased.

'I am not being fanciful,' I muttered through clenched teeth. 'Just you wait, Raoul Médoc, until the police find it. Then the laugh will be on you!'

'Enough, children! Enough!' Grandfather gestured us to silence. 'I wish that for once in a while you two would stop fighting each other the moment you meet.'

'Life would be very dull then,' Raoul's eyes twinkled teasingly. 'I like making Lucille angry. Anger makes her eyes sparkle like emeralds and she looks prettier than ever!'

'Oh!' I drew an indignant breath.

Grandfather chuckled. 'If you wish to pay compliments to my grand-daughter, Raoul, why not come and dine with us tonight?'

To my disappointment, Raoul shook his head. 'I wish I

could, Monsieur Verlaine, but hélas,' he shrugged, 'I have a previous engagement.'

'Never mind. There are plenty more evenings,' said my grandfather jovially. 'Your father tells me you are to be staying at home for a few weeks.'

'How are your parents, Raoul? Grandpère mentioned in one of his letters that your mother had been ill again.'

'Mother gets easily depressed. She hates living in Tourloup. There is so little to interest her here. I hope to persuade my father to take her elsewhere.'

'But we couldn't do without our good doctor!' protested Grandfather. 'Tourloup would not be the same without him. There would be no one for me to argue politics with, or to play chess with old Jules! In any case,' he went on, 'whom could we get to come in his place? No young man would want to set up practice and live so far from one of the big towns.'

'I think you may have to try,' said Raoul. 'My father – although don't mention this to anyone just yet – is seriously considering buying a small property at the coast, and retiring.'

Grandfather raised his eyebrows. 'He has never spoken to me of this intention.'

'It has been in his mind for some time, I can assure you,' said Raoul, 'but no doubt he doesn't even wish to tell you until his plans are more or less completed.'

'And will that be soon?'

'Who can say?' shrugged Raoul. 'There are so many factors to consider. But promise, Monsieur Verlaine, and you, too, Lucille, not to mention about this to a soul.'

'But, of course, we shall say nothing,' Grandfather answered for us both. 'And now, Raoul, if you will excuse us, it is high time we went along to the police station. As it is, Sergeant Duval won't be able to make much of a search of the river before darkness falls.'

Raoul said good-bye and hurried off, and Grandfather and I walked down the street and across the main square to the gendarmerie.

There I told Sergeant Duval my story, exactly as I had told it to my grandfather.

The Sergeant made careful notes and at the end of my recital, he shook his head.

'No one has been notified to me as missing in this district,' he said. 'Have you heard anything, Monsieur Verlaine?'

'No,' confirmed Grandfather. 'And as you are doubtless aware, Sergeant,' he went on, 'there is very little goes on in and around Tourloup that I don't hear about.'

'There haven't been many strangers about either,' said Duval thoughtfully. 'The recent bad weather has kept the usual influx of campers away.'

'And we are too far off the beaten track for casual tramps,' added Grandpère.

'How about Jules Lamartine? I haven't seen him about recently. He often fishes in the Lune, and he could have slipped and fallen in and no one any the wiser.'

'This man didn't have a beard, or I'd have mentioned it.'

'And I saw Jules in the distance this morning, taking his goats up the mountain.'

'Hmmph! Well, we'll just have to wait till we find the body, before we can tell who it is,' said Duval, standing up and putting away his notebook. 'If we need you again, I'll let you know, Miss Mathieson.'

I sighed with relief. The interview was over. I had done what Grandpapa called 'my civic duty' and now I could go home, and forget about the tragedy.

Martha, the housekeeper, was delighted to see me home again, and gave me a heart-warming welcome, but although she was all agog to know what had kept us late for supper, Grandfather insisted that we have our meal before we told her.

'Pauvre petite! What a homecoming,' observed Martha sympathetically, after she heard what had happened. 'But never mind, it is all over! From now, you can settle to enjoy your holiday.'

She gave me a sly look. 'Has Monsieur Verlaine got round to telling you Raoul Médoc is home just now?'

'He didn't need to tell me. We have already met!' I said. 'He is to be here for two or three weeks, I believe.'

'It was well planned, hein?'

'I don't know what you mean,' I blushed. 'He came home because his mother has not been well.'

'Pah! Madame Médoc is no more ill now than she has ever been, but it makes a good excuse!' Again she gave me a knowing look.

Grandfather jovially agreed. 'Young Raoul is not the type to leave the delights of Paris for the sake of a querulous mother! Like Martha, I think there is another attraction.'

'Go on, the pair of you! You are a couple of old match-makers!' I laughed. 'Raoul and I are old friends, nothing more.'

'You are twenty, Lucille. It is high time you thought of marriage,' said Grandfather pedantically.

'I certainly didn't spend three years studying at University just to get married at the end of it,' I objected.

'Just to get married!' echoed Martha indignantly. 'You speak as if marriage was something unworthy!'

'I didn't mean it that way,' I protested. 'But before I settle down there is so much I should like to accomplish.'

'And I still say young Médoc came home at this particular time for a particular purpose,' said Grandfather. 'He knew you would be here.'

'And I tell you, Grandpère, you have it all wrong!'

'No,' Grandfather shook his head. 'I overheard his mother tell the apothecary that Raoul was deeply interested in a young woman who lives here, and that was why, as much as for her sake, he had come home just now.'

'I'm not the only young woman in Tourloup,' I argued. 'Raoul has other girl friends,' but they wouldn't listen to me.

Later, when I went up to bed, and settled between the cool linen sheets, which smelt sweetly of lavender, I lay for a long time wondering if they were right.

Raoul Médoc would be considered a good match by most girls. He was clever and good-looking. His father was well thought of. His mother, a delicate, rather demanding woman, who kept poor Doctor Médoc running in circles round her, was elegant and handsome. And yet – well, Raoul for all his charm, could be difficult. Like his mother, he was inclined to be self-centred; he was also restless, ambitious, and had very high flying ideas – but then, I wasn't exactly perfect myself.

Of course, there was one important fact which neither Grandfather nor Martha knew, and which made me wonder if they were right about the reason for Raoul's presence in Tourloup at this time.

The last time I had seen Raoul, he had asked me to marry him, and I had refused. Had he come back to see if I would change my mind?

I feel asleep thinking of Raoul, but it was not Raoul I dreamed of. Instead, in my dreams I was back at the water meadow, staring down at the body of a man who floated in the river, but the face of the man was no longer the face of an unknown. It had changed into the dark, square, handsome face of the annoying young Scotsman who had come so near to crashing into me on the Col de la Lune!

When Martha came up next morning to waken me, I had had such a restless night I felt as if I had scarcely closed my eyes, and my tiredness made me quite crotchety.

I went down for breakfast dull-eyed and definitely not at my best, and my sour humour was not sweetened when Sergeant Duval called personally at the villa, his great bovine face split by a smile from ear to ear, to tell me that an hour earlier they had found a body, dressed as I had described, caught in a tangle of storm uprooted shrubs and broken branches at a bend in the river about a mile below the water meadow.

There was something about the Sergeant's grin which made me uneasy.

'What is so funny about finding a drowned man?' I asked sharply. 'You look as if it was a huge joke!'

'When you see your "corpse", you will think so too!' he grinned.

'What do you mean?' I demanded.

'What you took to be a drowned man, Mademoiselle Mathieson, was, thank goodness, no more than an old scarecrow! A suit of clothes, stuffed with straw round a stick, and a turnip head wedged on top!'

'No!' I denied sharply.

'Mais si!' said the Sergeant, and he started to laugh heartily. My grandfather joined in his mirth with his rumbustious bellow, so that the house echoed with merriment, making Martha come rushing in from the kitchen to see what it was all about.

Even Raoul Médoc, who had come to call, came in unannounced to see what the joke was, and he and Martha also joined in the laughter. But I didn't laugh.

It isn't that I can't take a joke against myself, but this time I saw nothing funny about the situation.

'I don't care what you found, Sergeant Duval!' I gritted my teeth in rage. 'What I saw was a body, and I shall prove it to you, even if I have to search the whole length of the river myself to find it!'

CHAPTER FOUR

By mid-morning the story had circulated round Tourloup and when I went down to the greengrocers for some peppers, I was chaffed so much by everyone I met that I got quite short-tempered.

The worst of it to my mind, however, was that I knew what I had seen had been no scarecrow. I may daydream at times, but on this event I had been wide awake, and you don't imagine staring eyes and a look of familiarity about a shapeless turnip, even if the colour of the skin hadn't been unlike that vegetable, with the upper part of the face browner than the lower part, a discolouration caused no doubt by hours of immersion in the water.

I tried to make Grandfather listen to me, but he broke into

chuckles whenever I broached the subject, and of course, I daren't approach Sergeant Duval again. Although he had been amused, he had ticked me off, half seriously, for wasting the time of the police.

For the rest of the morning, I went about like a bear with a sore head, even snapping at poor Martha, who took the huff and retired to the kitchen, leaving me to unpack my clothes myself instead of helping me do so while she gave me all the latest village gossip.

The drawers in the dressing-table had been lined with fresh newspaper, because Martha firmly believed that the smell of printer's ink deters moths from settling, and as I folded away my underwear and blouses, I filled in time by reading some of the old news items.

There was a bit about some starlet becoming an overnight success because of a film shown at the Cannes festival, with a photograph showing her posed on the beach in the merest suggestion of a bikini, and I wondered how Martha with her sense of what wasn't quite 'comme il faut' had not destroyed this blatant display of feminine charm, instead of framing it in my top drawer!

Another item, of local news this time, saying that the Villa des Lilas, the largest and most attractive house in Tourloup, had been bought by M. Albert Vincennes, the press lord, as a summer residence, interested me quite a bit. I had heard of Vincennes, a rags to riches millionaire who was reckoned a bit of a social climber and I wondered how he would react to the narrow social circle of Tourloup.

I opened another drawer, and here I found an item which, although only a small paragraph in a national paper, must have been of great interest to everyone in Tourloup, and I wondered why my grandfather had said nothing about it in his last letter.

Of course, it was possible that he had missed this particular piece of news, because it was tucked inconspicuously into a corner between an advertisement for Total petrol – 'votre bon génie', and Rexona (le seul savon déodorant au Déostérale!), and it informed the world that Major Heinrich

Haabe had been released that morning from a prison near Munich, where he had spent twenty years as a war criminal.

Heinrich Haabe had been the officer in charge of the German garrison at Tourloup, and it was he who had been responsible for the massacre in the Gorge de la Lune.

I read the paragraph twice, and almost went to ask Martha if she had known the news, but I decided against this. It was twenty-three years since the massacre. Why revive bitter memories?

I finished my unpacking and, feeling calmer and less sensitive to leg-pulling, I went down to the kitchen to restore good relationship with the housekeeper.

Harmony between us restored, I went into the garden to gather some anemones and lilies for the flower vases, and after lunch, I drove my car down to the garage to see my friend, Jacques, and ask him to mend the broken headlamp and touch up the scratch marks.

'You have been getting yourself into a lot of trouble these days, hein?' he grinned as he examined the damage. 'Still, nothing has been as bad as it seemed, and this,' he patted the wing, 'will be as easily restored to rights as a scarecrow!'

I grimaced at him. 'I want to hear no more of that!'

'When do you want your car?' he went on.

I shook my head. 'I don't expect I shall be using it for a day or so.'

'Good! I have another job on hand at the moment. Monsieur MacIntosh wants me to service his Alfa for him this afternoon.'

My jaw dropped. 'Oh! No!'

Jacques looked at me in surprise.

'What is the matter?'

'This Monsieur MacIntosh,' I asked. 'Is he about your height? Dark, sun-tanned—'

'Mais oui!' Jacques grinned. 'I see you have noticed him!'

I ignored the innuendo. 'I didn't realize he was staying in Tourloup.'

'Oh! You have met him before?'

'Yesterday!' I said grimly, indicating the damage to my

car. 'This is a memento of our meeting! But never mind that. Tell me, Jacques – is M. MacIntosh actually staying in Tourloup?'

'Si. At the Auberge de Mercredi.'

'Oh!' I considered this. I wasn't particularly anxious to meet the Alfa's driver again. He had sounded autocratic, ill-mannered and not at all my type, but if he was staying in Tourloup, with its one main thoroughfare, it was more than likely we would meet each other sometime.

'Is he staying for long?' I pried.

'That depends, I think, on the outcome of the survey,' Jacques told me.

'What survey?'

'Didn't your grandfather tell you? The authorities are thinking of making a roadway where the railway used to run. They say it would be an easy way for those motorists who go to Italy, who want to avoid the crowds on the N.7 between Mentone and Ventimiglia.'

'Why not simply re-open the railway line?'

'That wouldn't pay. Everybody goes by car these days – thank goodness!' he grinned. 'And think what it will do to my business if M. MacIntosh thinks the proposal feasible! I will make a small fortune with the last garage and petrol station before the frontier.'

'Don't count on it!'

'No. But it makes a pleasant dream – ah, and here comes M. MacIntosh himself!'

I looked round and saw the man I most wanted to avoid strolling towards me, and telling Jacques I would see him later, I hastily retreated along the road.

I had nothing in particular in mind planned for the afternoon, and as the way I was going led only to the outskirts of the village, dwindling off into the rough cart-track which led up towards Jules Lamartine's little shack, I decided, on the spur of the moment, to visit my old friend. The previous evening, Grandfather had told me Jules had been getting odder and odder as the winter months passed.

'He rarely comes into the village now, except for the

barest necessities and even then, his mind is in the clouds and he forgets who people are. Sometimes he acts as if we were all strangers, and last week, when I went to visit him, for old time's sake, with a flask of Martha's excellent soup and a bottle of Hennessy, he would not open the door to me.' All this my grandfather had said, but somehow I couldn't imagine Jules closing a door in my face.

He had always treated me as if I were a favourite niece, and there was a sympathy between us which I felt neither time nor illness would spoil and so I approached his cottage without fear of rebuff.

There was no sign of life about the shack, although Jules' two white goats stood tethered to a gnarled fig tree, from which they had long ago chewed the last vestige of green from the lower branches.

I knocked, and could have sworn I heard a rustle of movement inside, but when there was no reply to my summons, I decided that I had been mistaken and that the old man was not at home.

Jules is quite a character. He is tall and erect, and although he cares little for clothes, usually going around in any old suits which his friends hand over to him from time to time, he is very proud of his thick mane of white hair, which curls down over his shoulders, and his magnificent white beard, which makes him look more like a prophet from the Old Testament than a present day goatherd.

His is certainly not a figure one could miss, so I decided to go and look for him at one of his accustomed haunts up the mountainside or down by the river, where he might be spending the afternoon fishing. Since I hadn't seen him in the village itself, there was nowhere else he could be, because Tourloup is not the sort of place where you can miss seeing someone.

Before starting on my climb, I looked back at the village. Tourloup, like the other hill towns of the region, is not very big. It is perched high on the hillside of the Mont de la Lune and its only approach is by the road up which I had motored, and this road leads directly to the High Street and peters out on the spot where I was presently standing. It peters out, because there is nowhere for it to lead, for directly before me, for a mile or so, stretches steep rock, the track of an old glacier.

Save for a few brave clusters of rock roses and myrtle, this area is grey and forbidding. The glacier narrows up to and is cut off from the topmost heights of the mountain by a sheer precipice, which forms an impassable wall round the amphitheatre in which the village lies. On the other side of the village there is an equally sheer drop into the Gorge de la Lune. Before the war, the railway track had wound round the shoulder of the mountain, overlooking the gorge, but since it had been blown up during the war, Tourloup had been completely cut off from the east, and with only one approach road, liable in winter to be cut off by snow, I could understand why the local authorities were anxious to have the old railway line resurrected and made use of as a base for a new motor road. I could also understand how the destruction of this line had angered the Germans garrisoned in Tourloup during the war, because it left them with no back door to escape by in the event of an allied attack.

The only path leading to the top of the stone glacier is steep and worn to slippery smoothness, but occasionally it levels out, and where it does so, sheltered by boulders and the wall face itself, are table-cloth size patches of grass and wild mountain flowers where Jules takes his goats to feed. Still higher up, beside a narrow terrace, a few trees cling stubbornly to the rocky mountain face, giving shade for a strip of verdure where succulent mushrooms can often be gathered, but although I went hopefully from one patch of green to the next, there was no sign of the old hermit.

I took this to mean he must be down at the other end of the stony area where the River Lune has its origin. At this place, water flows from the rock into a deep pool, and from this pool a stream forms, which flows a few yards, disappears into a hole in the rock, and then emerges further down the hill to cascade in a glorious waterfall down on to the deep, dark gorge, whose sides rise smooth and sheer and insurmountable on either side of the young river. Jules loves to come her to meditate and water his goats, but again I drew a blank, so I made my way back up to the narrow goat track and from there, retraced my steps towards the shack.

As I approached the hut, I caught sight of the old man standing at a side window, his bearded face pressed against the dusty pane with a distorting result. He didn't see me at first, so I waved and shouted, whereupon he started back from the window and tugged the curtains together with an unfamiliar violence, shutting himself from view.

I ran up to the door and knocked.

'Jules!' I called. 'Jules! It's Lucille! Don't you recognize me?'

There was no reply.

'Come on, Jules! Let me in! I have so much to tell you.'

Still no reply, although I could hear the sound of breathing from the other side of the door.

'Please, Jules,' I coaxed, 'I will tell you about the art exhibition I went to see before I came here.' I tried the door handle with growing impatience, but the door was bolted against me.

With a final angry rattle, I called, 'I hope you will be more eager to see me when I come back tomorrow, Jules!' and I turned away.

So Grandfather had not been far wrong when he said Jules had gone a bit queer! Never in my life would I have expected this dear friend of mine to metaphorically slam his door in my face. The action was hurtful as well as puzzling.

Yes, and there was something else which puzzled me. Some thought which kept niggling at the back of my mind, but which I couldn't for the life of me bring into full focus.

What was it?

I hesitated, half turned to go back, then checked the impulse.

What good would it do me to return to the shack? Today, Jules was obviously not in the mood to see me. So I walked on, but still the feeling of unease persisted.

I was sure there was something important, something meaningful, behind Jules' peculiar actions which I had failed to comprehend, but the more I tried to fathom what it was that troubled my subconscious thoughts, the more muddled my reasoning became, and in the end I decided I must have been imagining things, and I continued on my way towards the village.

I didn't feel like going back home because Martha would be having her afternoon nap, and I didn't feel like following her example, so I walked down the High Street, blandly pretending not to notice the smiles and giggles which followed my progress.

The story of the body which turned into a scarecrow would amuse the community for days!

I think if my car hadn't been at the garage, I would then and there have driven to the spot on the river where I had sat the previous afternoon, and from there walked down the length of the river searching every possible place where my find might have been trapped, but I didn't want to go back to Jacques' place in case MacIntosh was still there, so instead I wandered along the path which led past Tourloup's famous violet farms, gathered some of the wild anemones I found by the wayside and went to place them on the base of the simple cross which marked the scene of the massacre of the Mercredi family and the resistance members of Tourloup in 1943.

For a long time I stood in the peaceful square of green by the river, reading the list of names which would pass into village history.

It was sad to think that the whole Mercredi family had been annihilated. The Mercredis were the grand seigneurs of the district. They had been liked by their workers and respected by everyone who came in contact with them. The old Comte had played an active part in the Resistance, under the very noses of the German Command, who had taken over all but a suite of rooms in the Chateau de Mercredi as their headquarters. His only son had been killed in the first days of the War, but his daughter-in-law and her two small sons, the future heirs of the estate, lived with him in the chateau.

Then came the dreadful day, after the sabotage of the railroad, when an informer had put the finger on the Comte for his part in the affair, and named all the others who had taken part, and that very day everyone then named, together with each member of the family, from the oldest to babes in arms, had been shot 'as a warning' by order of Colonel Heinrich Haabe.

After this, Haabe had calmly helped himself to the Mercredi treasures and although some of the valuable paintings and tapestries had since been recovered, the jewellery and gold and silver ornaments, worth about a quarter of a million pounds, were still missing.

Haabe's final act of vengeance on the Mercredis had taken place the day he left Tourloup when the Allies invaded Europe. Then he had set fire to the castle itself, and now, of the once beautiful building which had stood on a spur of rock dominating the entrance to the village, there remained only a blackened skeleton of stone.

'Daydreaming again, Miss Mathieson?' a mocking voice recalled me from my sad thoughts.

I started, turned to see who was speaking, and my heart beat faster with indignation as I stood once more face to face with Gregor MacIntosh.

CHAPTER FIVE

'I am sorry if we startled you, Miss Mathieson,' continued MacIntosh, amusement gleaming in his eyes as he saw me bite back the retort I would have made had he been alone, 'but you were lost in thought, weren't you?'

For a moment I did not answer him, because I was so busy looking at the girl who accompanied him.

She was exactly like a picture from the pages of *Vogue*.

Tall, sleek, hair styled to perfection round her oval face, make-up so cleverly applied it was scarcely noticeable – I had never before come in contact with anyone quite like her. As for her clothes, they would have cost at least a month of my income. Every seam, every tuck, every dart of the material spelled out 'Paris Collection'.

An elegant shirt, with deep cuffs at its elbow length sleeves, exactly matched the glowing champagne colour of the narrow belted, bell-bottom cotton trousers she wore, and the tan, slip-on shoes on her narrow, high-arched feet had the suppleness of real leather.

When I managed to take my eyes off the dark-haired beauty, I replied, simply.

'I was thinking how skin-deep our modern civilization is. All these families,' I indicated the list of names, 'wiped out by a supposedly educated man, from sheer, vengeful cruelty.'

'But it was all so long ago!' pouted MacIntosh's companion. 'And after all, there was a war on, and no one can fight, and win, wearing velvet gloves.'

As she spoke, in English as MacIntosh had done, but with an attractive French accent, her chestnut brown eyes swept over me, taking in every detail of my appearance from my wind-ruffled hair to the freckles the sun had coaxed out on my nose, and to the fact that the blouse and slacks I was wearing were last year's fashion.

'I don't expect you two girls have met before,' said MacIntosh, smiling from one to other of us. 'Annemarie, this is Miss Mathieson. Miss Mathieson, this is Madame Cordet.'

We acknowledged the introduction with politeness, but with the lack of enthusiasm which two women feel when they have decided to dislike each other on sight.

I instinctively resented the French girl, because she made me feel young and unworldly, and I think she did not respond to me because I was a woman and she had no time for women in general.

'Are you staying long in Tourloup, Madame Cordet?' I asked politely, 'or have you just driven up for the day?'

'In a way, I belong here,' she said to my surprise. 'My

father has bought a house here. For the summer months, you understand. Our real home is, naturally, Paris.'

'I thought town people preferred the coast in summer?'

'Father says the Cote D'Azur is too hot and crowded in July and August. Here we can have the best of both worlds, quietness or gaiety if need be. After all, the Mediterranean is only an hour's run from here by fast car.'

'Does your husband like it here?'

'I am a widow, Mademoiselle Mathieson,' she stated, and her eyes wandered to where MacIntosh stood, almost as if she were implying that her widowhood was not going to last long.

It was a 'hands off' signal, but she needn't have given it. My fellow countryman was about as unattractive to me as I was to him.

As if sensing our eyes on him, MacIntosh, who had been having a look at the memorial in front of which we were standing, said in his lilting Highland voice, 'How about yourself, Miss Mathieson? What brings you to such an out of the way place for a holiday?'

'I belong here more or less. Didn't you know?'

'You belong here!' he said incredulously. 'But your name! And your accent! I thought you were a Scot, like myself.'

It gave me a malicious feeling of pleasure to see him so taken aback.

'My grandfather is M. Verlaine, the solicitor,' I explained. 'If you have been here any length of time, you must have met him.'

'Of course,' MacIntosh's face lit up with understanding. 'How stupid of me! Only yesterday morning we were talking together and he told me he was expecting his granddaughter from England, but he didn't go into details and I took it for granted you were French, returning from college or from being an 'au pair' girl in Britain.'

'Didn't he even tell you my name? That should have told you.'

'Hardly,' he smiled. 'He referred to you as Lucille, and that was no indication of your true nationality, now was it?'

I puckered my brow. 'Then if you didn't know who I was, how did you know to introduce me to Madame Cordet as Miss Mathieson?'

He gave a sudden attractive grin. 'That was easy! I saw you leave the garage this afternoon, so when I went there I merely asked Jacques who the pretty blonde was!'

'Greg!' Feeling herself ignored for too long, Annemarie interrupted us, putting a possessive hand on MacIntosh's arm. 'I haven't all afternoon to chatter. We came down here to see the monument,' and she urged him forward to stand, with his back to me, facing the bold, stark memorial to the murdered sons and daughters of Tourloup.

I should have taken my dismissal gracefully and retreated from the spot, leaving them to enjoy the view on their own, but a nasty little streak of stubbornness in me urged me to linger on.

After all, I had been here first, so why should I go rushing away merely because an aggravating man and a supercilious young Parisienne wanted the quiet glade to themselves?

Consequently, instead of tactfully taking my leave, I, too, stepped back to the monument and started to re-arrange the anemones I had gathered earlier, and place them in a vase at the base of the sculpture.

All the time I was kneeling, fussing about my arrangement, I was conscious of Annemarie's annoyed glances, but Greg MacIntosh stood quietly, looking up at the pillar of stone, unaware of the silent duel of feminine personalities.

'This is hewn from the same rock as the walls of the gorge, isn't it?' he asked at length, running a finger exploringly over the surface of the stone. 'It's very simplicity is inspiring.'

'I don't see anything to it,' commented Annemarie. 'I can't understand why everyone who sees it praises it. I have seen prettier memorials in half the towns I have been in.'

'Monuments like this are not meant to be pretty,' the man reprimanded her. 'They are meant to make us feel.'

'Well, I can't say that this particular one inspires me with any great emotion,' she retorted sharply. 'It leaves me as cold as the stone it is sculpted from,' and she moved away as if impatient to be off.

MacIntosh was not to be hurried. He remained there, contemplating the memorial.

'You're wrong, Annemarie. The longer you look, the more you become aware of its austere beauty. You can sense what the artist was trying to convey, and yet,' he shook his head, 'it is difficult to imagine that this peaceful spot marks the scene of inhuman outrage.'

'You could say the same of Glencoe,' I commented.

'No!' MacIntosh shook his head in disagreement. 'There is a dark, brooding quality about Glencoe, but here,' his eyes wandered over the glade, from the craggy rock face on the far side of the stream, which glinted yellow in the afternoon sun, to the green pine grove which skirted the path leading to the main road above the meadow, and to the meadow itself, colourful as an artist's palette with the pinks of the honey-scented clover blossom and the saintfoin; the blues of the fragile bells of the campanulas, and the cream and golden drifts of meadow-sweet and marsh marigolds which covered the banks of the crystal clear Lune. 'Here,' he repeated, 'you simply can't imagine violence taking place here!'

I looked at him with new eyes, surprised by his vision.

'Viens!' said Annemarie impatiently. 'We have been here long enough. I have surveyed the monument and so I can tell everyone who asks me that this is so! I have done my duty to Tourloup. Now we can go, so that I can prepare for the party this evening.'

'A lot of preparing you'll do!' MacIntosh stepped towards her, smiling, his old self again. 'You will no doubt spend the rest of the afternoon wondering what to wear!'

Annemarie pouted prettily. 'That is not so, Greg. I may have to go to Castellane for some more cocktail savouries.'

'I'll take you, if you like.'

Annemarie's dimples showed as she smiled. 'If you will let me drive,' she wheedled.

'Oh, no!' Greg shook his head. 'No one drives my car but me! Especially not a woman!'

'Oh là!' Annemarie opened her eyes wide. 'This is ridiculous! Women drive every bit as well as men, do they not, Mlle Mathieson?' she turned to me to support her claim.

'I would say better than most,' I assured her, looking blandly at Greg. 'Why, only yesterday, a madman of a driver came racing down hill at the Col de la Lune, neither sounding his horn on corners, or giving sufficient berth to upcoming traffic. If I hadn't been competent, and done the right thing at the right time,' my mouth twitched with repressed laughter as I met Greg's indignant gaze, 'there would have been a very nasty accident.'

'You see!' Annemarie Cordet turned triumphantly to him, but Greg sneered and shook his head.

'No, Annemarie, I still hold my views. You see,' his eyes continued to hold mine, but I could not determine whether it was amusement or anger which sparked in them, so dead pan was his voice, 'only yesterday too, I was almost involved in an accident on the same stretch of road and this time it was a woman who wasn't sounding her horn, and who was cutting her corners.'

'I don't cut corners!' protested Annemarie.

'Nevertheless,' said Greg firmly, 'if you want me to go to Castellane with you, we go in my car and I drive.'

'Very well, Greg,' Annemarie capitulated gracefully, 'whatever you wish, naturellement!' she gave him a devastating smile, tucked her arm into his, and bidding me a disinterested 'Au revoir', together they strolled off towards the main road.

I watched them go, feeling unaccountably forlorn. At that moment, I almost wished I hadn't come back to Tourloup. It seemed I had run into nothing but trouble and unpleasantness since my return.

First, there had been my discovery at the river bank. Then there had been my near fatal accident on the hairpin bend, resulting in damage to my bright new Rapier, followed by the contretemps with Greg MacIntosh. After that, had come the police report that my 'body' had been nothing more tragic than a discarded scarecrow. I shuddered, remembering the laughter, at my expense, of Sergeant Duval, my grandfather and everyone who had been told the story. Even Raoul had found it very funny, although he hadn't gone as far as to say 'What did I tell you?'

I glared after the departing figures of Greg and Annemarie, not really seeing them, but rather all the people who had disbelieved me, because it *had* been a body I had found at the side of the river. In spite of the scarecrow 'evidence', I still had no doubts and all my unworthy friends would laugh on the other side of their faces when it eventually turned up and I was proved right.

Greg turned and gave me a final, friendly salute with his hand as he reached the roadway with his pretty companion, and for no good reason that I could think of this very gesture added to my feeling of woefulness.

Perhaps, I wondered, I felt this way because being a woman I was jealous of the French girl's beauty and kittenish – no, I amended – feline charm. Or perhaps I was annoyed with Greg MacIntosh for his arrogant assumption that man was superior to woman in all things. Or again, and this time I felt I was getting nearer the mark, perhaps it was because there was no handsome young man I could gaily ogle, as Annemarie had gaily ogled Greg, and no man who would take my arm with the assured possessiveness with which Greg had taken Annemarie's.

I kicked disconsolately at a tuft of coarse grass in front of me. For someone who prided herself on having her emotional house in order, I could not understand the way my mind was working and, feeling quite downcast, I slowly began to trudge up the steep path towards the road which Greg and Annemarie had taken a couple of minutes earlier.

The sound of a nearby gunshot, which sent the wood pigeons wheeling and fluttering among the tree tops, interrupted my mournful thoughts and made me jerk forward with a start which caused me to trip over the exposed ground root of a pine tree which stretched across the path.

I tried to regain my balance but the steep path was rubbed so smooth with constant traffic that I could not keep my footing, and I slipped and fell forward on my face, at the very moment that another shot rang out and something which sounded vaguely like an angry hornet, but which travelled much faster, cut through the air where my head had been seconds earlier and hit the trunk of the pine tree above me with a smart rap.

CHAPTER SIX

'Attention!' I screamed, pushing myself up a few inches. 'You! You with the gun! Have a care! There is someone down here!'

No one answered. All I could hear was the anxious fluttering of the birds overhead, and the frightened beating of my own heart.

I scrambled to my feet, hastily brushing away a trickle of blood from my forehead, and started to run up the path towards the main road, which I reached in seconds, hot, breathless and in a flaming temper.

If I could get hold of the madman with the gun I would give him a piece of my mind, I vowed, as I peered angrily this way and that down through the trees and along the road, but the only people in view were Greg MacIntosh and Annemarie Cordet, who were strolling slowly along some two hundred yards or so ahead of me towards the village.

I went hurrying after them, and at the sound of my approaching footsteps, they both looked round.

'Mr MacIntosh, Mme Cordet,' I cried. 'Have you seen anyone with a gun?'

Greg stared at me in surprise. 'Miss Mathieson, you look upset. What has happened?'

'Someone nearly killed me!' I said, and in spite of myself, my voice wobbled nervously.

'You're imagining things!' exclaimed Annemarie.

I shook my head. 'When I was coming up the pathway from the monument, some idiot was shooting at pigeons in the wood. It was only by the grace of my patron saint that I didn't end up a dead bird myself.'

I clenched my fists and gritted my teeth to control rising hysteria.

'Your head is bleeding!' exclaimed Annemarie. 'Were you actually hit?'

'No!' I couldn't repress a shiver. 'But if I hadn't tripped over a tree root and fallen, I might well have been.' I brushed away another annoying trickle of blood from my brow. 'A bullet just missed me by inches.'

'Come, Miss Mathieson,' Greg MacIntosh admonished me. 'You have had a scare no doubt, but I'm sure there wasn't a shot within yards of you!' He smiled annoyingly. 'Anyone out after pigeons would be more likely to aim towards the tree tops than among the trunks.'

Hysteria gave way to rage.

'I'm getting tired of people in Tourloup not believing what I say!' I said angrily. 'This time I should like to prove myself right. Come!' I caught at his arm. 'I shall show you just what a narrow escape I had.'

MacIntosh tried to withdraw his arm.

'Very well, Miss Mathieson. I believe you,' he eventually conceded, but his tone was still doubtful and it added to my anger.

'No!' I said firmly. 'You don't. But you will have to believe the evidence of your own eyes. Come!' I urged him.

'Well—' he looked at Annemarie.

'It won't take minutes,' I said quickly.

'All right then. If it will make you feel better,' Greg reluctantly gave in.

'Annemarie, if you don't mind waiting here for me, I promise I shall only be gone for five minutes.'

'Oh, no!' said Annemarie sharply. 'If there does happen to be an idiot with a gun on the loose, I am not staying here on my own! I am coming with you,' and with that she once more took hold of Greg MacIntosh's arm, glaring at me as she did so, almost as if she suspected I had made up my tale to get him to myself.

In about three minutes, we were back on the path leading down to the memorial, and Greg had to admit that he could not ascribe to my imagination the bullet wound about five feet up in the trunk of the pine tree, and the fact that the shot was of very recent origin was emphasized by the fresh resin which was beginning to ooze from the hole.

'You did have a lucky escape!' said MacIntosh grimly, looking from the scarred bark to the marks on the path which indicated where I had slipped and fallen. 'If you had been standing upright, that shot might have hit you!'

His lips tightened. 'It was downright dangerous to shoot so low. I think we should go along and have a word with your village policeman.'

'What good would that do?' I asked sourly. 'The pigeon shooter isn't likely to own up to his negligence. I only brought you here to prove what I had said was true.'

'All the same, I think the police should be told.'

'No, no,' I demurred. 'In any case, Sergeant Duval would probably treat it as a joke!'

'I don't see why he should,' objected Greg, and at his words, I gave a little inward sigh of relief, because they pointed to the fact that he had not heard of the amusement I had already caused in the village, and I hoped he never would hear, because his opinion of me was low enough as it was.

Annemarie moved impatiently.

'Miss Mathieson is right, Greg, so why waste any more time? After all, what good would it do to lodge a complaint with the police when there is no one to complain about?'

She tugged at his arm. 'One thing, we shall know not to go strolling in these woods again.' She gave an involuntary shiver. 'Come on, let's get away from here.'

I couldn't have agreed with her more, for now the glade, which half an hour ago had seemed so innocent and peaceful, had assumed a menacing quality and I wanted to be away from it.

I glanced about me nervously. Somehow, I had the peculiar impression that we were not alone here; that someone was watching us; someone who boded no good.

Instinctively I moved a little closer to Greg MacIntosh.

Whether he was aware of my feeling of unease, or whether in his naturally arrogant manner he automatically assumed the male role of protector to the weaker sex, Greg responded to my movement by firmly taking my arm.

'You have had a bit of a shake-up, Miss Mathieson, and no wonder,' he observed. 'Annemarie and I shall see you safely to your home,' he gently urged us up the path, 'but there is one thing you must promise me. Even if you persist in saying nothing to the police, you will mention this incident to your grandfather. M. Verlaine is a wise man and he knows most of the inhabitants of Tourloup. I wouldn't be at all surprised if he has a good idea who was fooling around, and to whom to give a private word of warning.'

By this time we had again reached the main road and all together we walked smartly up the High Street to the Villa Beau Site. Not until we were actually at the front door did Greg relinquish his hold of my arm.

'Here we are,' he announced. 'And, Miss Mathieson, remember what I said about telling your grandfather.'

I nodded. 'I'll tell him.'

'Good. Then good-bye – and see you take care of yourself!' he added in a surprisingly kindly tone.

'Au revoir, Mademoiselle Mathieson,' said Annemarie, still possessively clinging to Greg's other arm. 'A ce soir!'

I wondered what she meant by that, but before I could ask, she was urging her companion away and as they left me, I heard her tell him they really would have to get a move on, if they were to get to Castellane and back before six o'clock.

I walked slowly up the path and through the beaded curtain which screened the open front door, and I was hardly conscious of the throbbing in my head or the tight discomfort of the blood which had dried on my brow. I was too busy thinking of the past minutes; too aware of the lingering pressure from Greg MacIntosh's firm grip on my right arm.

Tentatively, with my fingertips, I touched the area where he had held me.

For the past few years, I had become so used to looking after myself, except for the brief holiday periods when Grandfather and Martha fussed over me, that I found it odd to be treated protectively by anyone, and particularly by someone who rather annoyed me and to whom I seemed to be equally annoying.

Martha heard my footsteps in the hall, and called from the kitchen, where I went to join her to see what she was preparing for our evening meal.

'Lucille, mon enfant! Qu'est-ce qu'il y a? What have you been doing to yourself?' she exclaimed anxiously, when she saw the mark on my forehead and the dusty patches on the knees of my slacks.

Briefly, I explained what had happened.

Her lips tightened into an angry line.

'I'll bet it was that Marcel!' she decided. 'He is always up to some foolish caper or another, and I have lived in dread of what might happen since his doting parents gave him a sporting gun for his birthday.'

With that, she hurried off to the medicine cupboard to return a minute or two later with a wad of cotton wool, and a bottle of some potion which she herself had distilled from a variety of herbs and which she believed to be a veritable panacea.

Martha bathed the scratch on my forehead with hot water, and when it was clean enough for her liking, she dabbed it carefully with the potion, ignoring my indrawn breaths when the liquid stung my flesh.

'Là!' she said eventually. 'That should do it.'

She stood back to survey her handiwork. 'I do hope it will not leave a scar,' she frowned. 'Certainly, for tonight, you will have to be very skilful with your make-up to hide the blemish.'

I selected an apple from the basket on the kitchen table and bit into it.

'What is so special about tonight?' I asked. 'Has Grandpapa asked someone for supper?'

Martha's eyes rounded in astonishment.

'Surely you know where you are going tonight!' she exclaimed. 'Or did M. Verlaine forget to mention it?'

'Mention what?' I demanded, my pulse quickening with suspicion.

'Zut alors!' Martha shook her head. 'How like a man! Don't you know you have been asked to attend at the cocktail party this evening at the Villa des Lilas? That is why I am preparing an early supper!'

'Oh!' I exclaimed happily. 'I didn't know I had been asked to the party! But that would explain why Madame Cordet said 'A ce soir', when she left me just now.'

'Madame Cordet?' asked Martha. 'You already know her?' She looked at me with her sharp, curious button eyes. 'What is she like?'

'Have you never seen her?' I said in surprise.

'Of course, I have seen her!' said Martha drily. 'One could hardly help that! She and her father have been living in Tourloup since the beginning of June, and Madame Cordet is not a woman one could overlook! No, what I mean is, what is she like as a person?'

'She seems all right,' I said without great enthusiasm. 'But she is very beautiful, isn't she? And her clothes!' I shook my head with a sigh. 'They make me green with envy!'

Martha nodded. 'I dare say, but clothes aren't everything.' She added a dash of spice to a pot on the stove. 'I have heard she is none too popular with the women here, but with the men, that is a different matter!'

She shook her head reprovingly. 'A number of husbands have been told to keep their eyes away from her!'

'I wonder what made them come to Tourloup of all places?' I queried. 'There are other quiet hilltop villages in the region which are much more convenient for trips down to the coast.'

'Raoul Médoc had something to do with it, so I believe,' Martha gave me an appraising look. 'It appears he was a friend of Madame Cordet's late husband, and when he heard that M. Vincennes, Mme Corbet's father, was looking for a suitable holiday villa in this area, he talked him into buying the Villa des Lilas.'

'Oh!'

'Yes,' she nodded, adding as an afterthought, 'Raoul Médoc could talk almost anyone into doing anything when he decides to be charming. I think that is why he is so successful as a Paris society columnist.'

'He can't talk me into anything I don't want!' I said wickedly.

Martha looked aggrieved. She has a soft spot for Raoul, with whom I have been friends since childhood.

I also know that Grandpapa and Doctor Médoc would both like to see this friendship develop into something deeper, but in the past, whenever Raoul has shown signs that he thinks the same, I have taken cold feet and denied him the opportunity of pinning me down to a definite understanding. Martha must have guessed something of my thoughts.

'Maybe you are not as clever as you think,' she said, looking at me slyly over the pot of soup she was stirring. 'It is not difficult to see that Madame Cordet has an eye on your friend!'

'Bah!' I laughed. 'That young woman would set her cap at any man!'

'Perhaps so, but there is something in the way she looks at your Raoul which makes me uneasy.' She paused to taste the bouillon. 'They are two of a kind, you must understand. Both good-looking, sophisticated, fond of the gay life – yes!' she nodded wisely. 'It is obvious to me they have much in common, and a woman of thirty, who has been once married, feels the lack of a husband more than a spinster—'

I interrupted her, laughing.

'Go on with you, Martha! Are you trying to tell me that Madame Cordet has honourable intentions towards Raoul?' I giggled. 'Honestly! I can't believe it! For one thing,' I thought of Annemarie's model clothes and the glittering rings on her fingers, 'Raoul, with his journalist's pay, would never be able to keep her in the luxury to which she is obviously accustomed, and for another, I doubt if the lovely widow would like to live in what to her would be reduced circumstances.'

'Madame Cordet is a wealthy woman in her own right, so I understand,' said Martha, 'so these things would not matter. I thought I ought to give you fair warning, though. You have kept Raoul at arm's length for too long. He may have decided to accept someone else's embrace!'

'Away with you!' I said, flinging the apple core into the waste bin. 'I am sure you are exaggerating the friendship to try and bring me to heel!' I smiled fondly at her.

'Now, tell me, what do you think I should wear this evening to compete with my rival – that is, if you are quite sure I have been invited to her party!'

'Of course, you have been invited,' said Martha. 'Everyone who is anyone in Tourloup and district has been invited, to say nothing of people from as far away as Nice and Cannes and Monte Carlo! At least, that is what I have been told by Thérèse Lebrun and she should know, because she has been engaged as housekeeper by M. Vincennes.'

'Gosh!' I exclaimed. 'It's going to be some party, isn't it? There will be plenty of excitement in Tourloup tonight.'

'Si, si!' agreed Martha. 'Poor Sergeant Duval will have quite a headache controlling all the cars that will converge on the Villa des Lilas! It's just as well,' she went on with a hint of malice, getting her own back because I wouldn't be serious about Raoul, 'that it was only a scarecrow you saw in the Lune, otherwise he really wouldn't have known how to cope!'

'Oh, Martha!' I grimaced. 'I've heard enough about that scarecrow for one day.'

Martha smiled. 'You should be grateful to Madame Cordet, then! She has saved you a lot of embarrassment, because her party tonight is the main topic of conversation and your amusing error has been relegated to the background.'

Martha's words made me thoughtful, not so much because

of what she had said about my supposed error, but because of what she had said about Raoul.

Annemarie Cordet appeared, at the moment, to be the central figure of attraction in Tourloup, and knowing Raoul Médoc as I did, I wasn't too surprised that he was playing up to her.

Raoul is like a garden moth, in more ways than one. He likes to come out at night and he is attracted by bright lights. Where the flame shines, he is inclined to flutter.

All the same, I determined, if the pretty Parisienne thought she was going to annexe him, she was in for a disappointment. After all, she had Greg MacIntosh on a string, so that should suffice her. She wasn't going to have my old friend, too!

So, I smiled to myself, I would be especially nice to Raoul this holiday and wean him from Annemarie's charms, because Madame Cordet, with her pretty, pouting ways, and her predatory fingers clutching at every man's sleeve, was not going to leave me partnerless on my own home ground!

CHAPTER SEVEN

I knew I couldn't compete with Annemarie Cordet as a beauty, but at least I could make the best of what good points I had.

Since the only advantage I reckoned I had over Annemarie was in the matter of age – a full nine years of it – I decided to offset the petite Parisienne's beauty box glamour and sophistication with youthful naturalness and unworldliness.

I studied myself attentively in the clear mirror of the bedroom dressing-table.

My green eyes, like those of my grandfather's tabby cat, had an amber glint in their depths, and might be considered my one claim to beauty. My skin is fair and the sun had brought out a sprinkling of tiny freckles on my nose, but it is smooth and soft to the touch, like peach bloom. My mouth is slightly crooked, and gives my smile a lop-sided look, which Raoul had once told me he found attractively provocative, and my hair . . .

I looked at it and sighed. I would certainly have to do something about it before tonight's cocktail party, for after my afternoon's adventure, it was dusty and matted above the brow with dried blood from the scratch and an excess of Martha's wonderful potion. I spent the next half-hour washing and setting it, and I was pinning in the last plastic roller, when I heard Grandfather arrive back from the office.

Before I could go down from the bedroom to greet him, I heard Martha hurry from the kitchen and start to tell him, with a great deal of exaggeration, about my afternoon's misadventure.

'What is more, M. Verlaine,' I heard her say as I reached the hall, 'I am sure it was that Marcel who did the shooting.'

'We mustn't jump to conclusions like that!' said Grandfather judiciously. 'As it happens, I know that Marcel and his parents are off to Grenoble today.' He frowned. 'All the same, I wonder who it could have been? It doesn't sound like any of the pigeon shooters I know.'

'Let's not talk about it any more,' I entered the conversation. 'Someone made a mistake, which probably scared him as much as it did me, and it will probably be a sharp lesson to him to be more careful in future.'

I took him by the arm and led him into the lounge. 'Now,' I remarked brightly, 'tell me, Grandpère, why didn't you tell me about the cocktail party we have been invited to this evening. Or about the new people at the Villa des Lilas?'

'Your "find" yesterday put all these thoughts from my head,' he replied. 'When I did remember about the invitation, after lunch today, you had already gone out for a walk.'

'Oh, yes! That reminds me,' I released Grandfather's arm

and went to sit by the window where my hair would dry in the sun. 'I went to see Jules this afternoon.'

'So!' Grandfather paused in the act of lighting a cigarette. 'You went to see Jules, hein? Did you see him?' he eyed me keenly.

'No. I didn't, as a matter of fact, although I am quite sure he was at home.'

Grandpapa nodded knowingly. 'I'm not surprised. Jules has been acting very oddly of late.'

'What do you mean?'

'Over the years, Jules has become more and more of a hermit. You and I and Doctor Médoc are the only ones he has encouraged about his shack. You – not only because you are your father's daughter, but because, as he himself told me once, you were the only girl, young woman, indeed, who did not shrink back when he saluted you with the mutilated stumps which were his hands.

'Latterly, you see, as age shrivelled the skin on his limbs, as it does on us all as we grow older, I think he became ever more conscious of their unsightliness.'

'But why should anyone shrink from his touch?' I cried. 'He is so gentle! Anyway, as far as I am concerned I have always regarded his disfigurement as something for him to be proud of! A greater emblem of courage than his Croix de Guerre.'

'I am afraid you are unique in that respect, Lucille. Other people, especially those of your own generation, who know nothing of what we went through, don't see it that way,' said Grandpapa sadly. 'As for his contemporaries, for the most part they are so occupied with the business of running their own lives, they have forgotten or relegated to the background of their memory, the fact that if Jules Lamartine hadn't remained silent under torture, they might be lying, with their families, under the monument by the river along with the last of the Mercredis and those others, whom a lesser man betrayed.'

'It was one of the gardeners at the Castle who played the traitor, wasn't it?'

'Some say that. Others think it was the wife of Mathieu, the apothecary, who was supposed to have been more than friendly with Major Haabe's aide. But whoever it was, treacherous servant or faithless wife, it did not matter, because both of them were killed in the massacre for which they had been responsible.'

'What I could never understand, Grandpapa, is how neither you, nor Jules, nor your other associates were included in that list of Resistance workers?'

'That is easily answered, chérie. There were two groups working in this area, a fact known only to Mercredi and myself. It was Mercredi's group, which incidentally was the one to which the apothecary was attached, which was betrayed.'

I gave a little shiver.

'I don't know how you had the nerve to carry on after that!'

'Nerve, my dear? I don't think it was so much courage as hatred and defiance which kept us going. The Bosche had tried to bring us to our knees, and we meant to show him that the people of these mountain regions can never be wholly conquered!'

There was a far-away look in his eyes as he finished speaking and for several minutes he stood, staring out across the flagged terrace, out beyond the gorge which cut off our garden from the far bank of the Lune, out over the mountains which dipped gradually lower and lower to the shores of the Mediterranean Sea.

But it was not the view he was seeing. I sensed he was back in the past, reliving the old, dangerous days and mourning anew those who, unlike himself, could no more enjoy the maquis scented mountain air on their faces, or the benison of the sun's touch on their cheeks.

'You were telling me about Jules,' I gently broke the spell of silence and brought him back to the present.

'About Jules?' he repeated vaguely. 'Oh, yes! Of course! We were discussing Jules Lamartine, weren't we?' He paused.

'Well, as I was saying, Lamartine seems to have grown very odd of late. He avoids his fellows more and more, and he is even beginning to imagine things.'

'What kind of things?' I prompted.

'For instance, when I went to see him at the beginning of last week, he was very excited. He said he had seen men digging among the ruins of the old chateau, and along the embankment of the railway line. He went to challenge them and immediately they vanished from view!'

Grandfather shook his hand. 'I tried to calm him. I explained that there were men digging along the embankment, because there was a scheme in hand to clear the track, blast away the rock falls which had put it out of commission, and restore the old line as a modern motor road into Italy, but he would have none of that.

' "No! No!" he denied this angrily. "It wasn't the labourers for the roadworks I saw, unless they were working at midnight with masked torches! Non, Verlaine. These men I saw were not members of the road gang. There was something odd about them! Something very odd is going on here!" '

Grandfather sighed. 'I tried to quieten him down and make some sense out of what he was saying, but his mind seemed to wander. He stared at his hands in a way that made my blood run cold, and he started to shake as if with ague, and mumble away, "You will never get what you want! Never! Never!"

'It was frightening, Lucille. His mind had jumped back a quarter of a century and he was back in prison, defying the Nazis. I left him then, and he scarcely noticed my going,' Grandfather concluded sadly.

'But why wouldn't he see me?' I persisted. 'Do you think he didn't know who I was?'

'That could be. Actually, I myself tried to see him the day before you came home, to tell him about your holiday, but although I knocked and shouted for him, he simply would not open the door to me. There was another thing too,' he frowned. 'I noticed, as I stood there, that he had not even milked his goats that day. The poor creatures looked downright miserable and neglected.'

'That doesn't sound in the least like Jules!' I exclaimed. 'I have never known him to be unkind or thoughtless to a living creature in all my life.'

'That, as much as anything else, is what convinces me that our old friend is becoming a bit,' he tapped his head significantly, 'and incapable of looking after himself any more.'

'Is there anything we could do to help him?'

'One day, and that fairly soon, I'm afraid, something will have to be done about him,' said Grandfather gravely.

'Oh, no!' I protested, reading what was in his mind. 'You wouldn't condemn him to an institution! Debarred of the freedom which he prizes so much, he really would go mad!'

I touched Grandpapa's arm. 'He isn't doing anyone any harm, is he?' I pleaded. 'Don't you think it would be kinder simply to leave him alone? After all,' I argued, 'there is no law against one's keeping oneself to oneself, is there?'

'My dear Lucille,' he replied gently, 'I understand only too well how you feel, but one must beware of pity. We must not let sentiment blind us to reason. Nine times out of ten,' he said slowly, 'sentiment is the coward's excuse for not doing something which ought to be done, but which is unpleasant to do.'

'But, Grandpère, an institution! Is there nothing else that can be done? After all,' I said hopefully, 'perhaps Jules is acting like this because he isn't feeling well and does not wish to impose himself on anyone. Yes,' I continued firmly, 'I am sure that is it!' I strummed my fingers thoughtfully on the rail of the balustrade against which I was leaning. 'I know. I shall ask Raoul to tell his father to look in on Jules.'

Grandfather heaved a sigh.

'I'm afraid that is no good either, Lucille. You see, Doctor Médoc called on him the day after I told him about Jules' midnight diggers, and he, too, had the door slammed in his face for his pains.

'Yes,' he continued, 'it is a difficult situation – but enough of that for the moment,' he said more briskly. 'If we are to dine before going to the Villa des Lilas this evening, we have not much time to waste!'

I lingered in the evening sunshine.

'Tell me, Grandpapa, what is our host, Monsieur Vincennes, like?'

He shrugged.

'Vincennes is quite a likeable character, even if he isn't exactly my type. He's very commercial minded, with money his main topic of conversation, but he does try to be friendly and it is obvious he wishes to fit into the village life.

'Of course, as you can imagine, there are all sorts of rumours about his origin, and how his money was made in the black market after the war, but no sensible person listens to tales like these. As you know, strangers are always suspect to the Tourloup man-in-the-street.'

Grandfather moved towards the lounge and I followed.

'Speaking for myself,' he continued, 'I am glad to see the Villa des Lilas lived in again after all these years. It is too fine a house in a splendid setting to go to waste, and Monsieur Vincennes has spared no money in making it as lovely and luxurious a home as any along the Riviera itself. What is more, he employed mainly local labour and local craftsmen and local tradesmen to do the renovations, and this has gone a long way towards making him acceptable to the community.'

'His daughter is very beautiful,' I remarked casually. 'Martha tells me Raoul appears to be interested in that direction.'

I covertly watched for Grandpère's reaction to this statement.

There was the briefest of pauses before he replied.

'All young men are interested in a pretty woman. It is only natural. Moreover, in the case of Raoul Médoc and Madame Cordet, I understand Raoul was a friend of her late husband's and that they have a number of mutual acquaintances in Paris, so it is not to be wondered at if they see each other frequently in Tourloup.'

'Do you think Raoul followed her from Paris?' I probed.

'The Médocs knew you were coming here this month,' he countered, blandly ignoring my question.

Further conversation was interrupted by Martha sounding the gong to announce that supper was ready, and since she hates to be kept waiting, and since Grandfather does not believe in table talk, no more was said on the subject until Grandpapa selected his after dinner cigar, cut it with due care, lit it, and slowly savoured the first satisfying inhalation.

'You know, Lucille, I shouldn't worry too much about Raoul and Madame Cordet,' he pronounced meditatively. 'Raoul is not the only eligible young man in the district. Madame Cordet casts a wide net.'

'With a narrow mesh!' I added, half amused, half annoyed. 'I don't think she minds what she catches, so long as it is male!'

Grandfather laughed. 'Don't be so cynical, chérie. It is the way she is made. In any case, there are always the clever ones who slip away in time!' He stood up and patted me on the shoulder.

'I'd back you against a dozen Madame Cordets, if it came to the pitch,' he assured me. 'There are things other than beauty, or worldly wealth, which a worthwhile man looks for in a wife.'

'Such as a fiery temper?' I said with wry humour, acknowledging my chief fault.

'Such as an ability to laugh at oneself, and be loyal to one's friends!' He gave me a gentle shove.

'Now off with you and get dressed for the occasion. We are expected at the Villa des Lilas in less than an hour!'

CHAPTER EIGHT

By the time I had had a bath, and finally decided what I was going to wear, my hair was dry and I was able to remove the rollers and brush it out.

Martha came up to the bedroom to see if she could help me with anything, and while I took the dress I was going to put on from the wardrobe and laid it carefully on the bed, she fussed around, making sure my stockings were neither snagged nor laddered, that my high-heeled evening sandals were immaculate.

Then when I was ready for it, she carefully slipped the short, white silk cocktail dress over my head, and pinned my lingerie straps out of sight along the shoulder seam.

Thereafter she waited patiently while I sat down at the dressing-table and brushed my hair until it gleamed like ripe barley in the sunlight, and arranged it in a youthful, shoulder-length, page-boy style. When I had it arranged to my satisfaction, Martha sprayed it all over with a mist of lacquer to ensure that not one single tendril would escape the invisible net.

After this was done I applied some pancake make-up to the scar on my brow and gently rubbed it in to camouflage the blemish. A dusting of face powder, a skilful deepening of the colour of my lips with a cerise lip salve, and I stood up and faced Martha to ask her critical judgment.

She gave me a slyly approving look, but said merely.

'You'll do!'

She picked up my evening bag, put in a fresh handkerchief, handed it to me, and then said, 'Un moment! You almost forgot this!'

She lifted up my perfume atomizer, and pressed it to release a cloud of delicate flower scent round my neck and wrists and hair line.

'Voilà!' She gave me another critical glance. 'Thank

goodness the scratch on your brow does not show,' and with that she urged me gently from the bedroom.

Grandfather, looking very big and broad and important in his rarely worn evening suit, was waiting for me at the foot of the stairs, and the look of approval in his eyes, as he watched me descend, told me he admired my simple, white, sleeveless dress, and the dainty necklet of fine gold chain with its pendant of star peridot set in seed pearls, which was the only jewellery I wore.

'How pretty you look, child!' he beamed. 'And how youthful! I can see that even the beautiful Madame Cordet will have to look to her laurels this evening!'

Proudly he took me by the arm, to escort me from the house.

'Have a pleasant time!' Martha wished us, as she came to stand in the doorway to see us off. 'You can tell me all about the affair tomorrow.'

Spring had come late to the Alpes Maritimes this year and summer was not yet in full stride, and so the lilac trees which hedged the drive-way, and from which the Vincennes' villa derived its name, were still in bloom.

In the light of the gay Chinese lanterns which swung from the boughs, the plumes of the flower-heads gleamed wax-like and unreal, but there was nothing unreal about the headiness of their perfume, and I sniffed appreciatively at the scented air as, arm in arm with my grandfather, I strolled sedately to the curving path which led to the front door.

Since our house was little more than a stone's throw from the Villa des Lilas, there had naturally been no necessity for us to take the car. We were lucky in this respect, because by the time we arrived, there was not a parking place to be seen for about a couple of hundred yards on either side of the gateway, and cars were still arriving.

I could see a fine traffic jam building up along the Col de la Lune when the party was over, and I did not envy Sergeant Duval his task of having to cope with it!

'I had not realized the party tonight was to be such a big

affair,' observed my grandfather. 'I wonder where on earth everyone is going to be accommodated!'

We had our answer to this when we arrived and were directed down a flight of steps to the basement. What had once been a number of large cellars beneath the villa, had been transformed into a long, low ceilinged ballroom, with gleaming parquetry flooring. At one end of the room was a well stocked bar, where a small man in a white jacket was serving drinks, and in a deep alcove at the other end a band was playing soft, discreet, background music.

The wall on the entire length of the house on the right-hand side had been taken away, and three great, double-glazed plate glass windows installed in its place.

In the daytime, the view over the gorge and the rolling hills beyond must have been superb. Even now, with the bright moonlight touching the mountain peaks with silver, and emphasizing the black profundity of the deep clift through which the river ran, it was breath-taking.

Monsieur Vincennes, our host, and his daughter, were standing in the middle of the room to welcome their guests.

As we approached them, I noticed, with a twinkle of amusement, that like all the other male guests, my grandfather was subjected to the full battery of Annemarie's charm, from the fluttering eyelashes to the huskily caressing voice of welcome.

Her attitude to me was not quite so enthusiastic!

Madame Cordet's eyes had narrowed speculatively as she gave me a swift look over, which took in every detail of my appearance, and then with a sweet note of sympathy, whose falseness only I appreciated, she said,

'I am so glad you were able to come tonight, Mademoiselle Mathieson, and,' her eyes fastened on my brow, 'more than glad that your unfortunate fall this afternoon has not left too noticeable a blemish on your forehead.'

Immediately the eyes of everyone within earshot focused on my brow and I flushed self-consciously.

I wanted to make an equally acid-sweet reply, but Grand-papa, knowing my disposition, put his hand on my elbow and urged me past Annemarie to introduce me to her father.

'So you are the lovely grand-daughter Monsieur Verlaine has been boasting about!'

My host's genial greeting made up for his daughter's deflating sweetness. He held out his hand.

'I have been looking forward to meeting you, Mademoiselle, and I am also sure that Annemarie will be delighted at having someone like you for a companion here in Tourloup. Is that not so, chérie?' He turned to his daughter.

'Bien sur, Papa!' said Madame Cordet, but the sweetness of her smile did not reach her eyes.

I turned back to Monsieur Vincennes.

'Grandfather has been telling me about the renovations you have carried out in the villa,' I tactfully switched to a safe ground for conversation, and Grandpapa nodded in relief. 'If this ballroom is anything to go on,' I continued, 'the rest of the house must be superb.'

'You must let me show you over the villa some day soon,' my host responded with obvious delight at my interest. 'I planned all the alterations myself, although Annemarie, with the help of her good friend, Raoul Médoc, is responsible for the choice of furnishings.'

'Did I hear someone mention my name?' Raoul himself materialized at my side.

'Ah! Raoul! Have you met Mademoiselle Mathieson?' asked Monsieur Vincennes.

'Lucille and I have been friends since as far back as I can remember,' smiled Raoul.

'Then perhaps you could introduce her to some of Annemarie's young friends who are here tonight while I have a word with Monsieur Verlaine?'

'Bien sur!' said Raoul cheerfully. 'It will be a pleasure!'

He led me across the floor towards a chattering group of elegantly dressed young people, who were crowding round the bar.

Madame Cordet made to follow us, but her father caught her arm.

'Ah! Here are your friends the Cartiers, Annemarie! How

good of them to come such a distance, especially when Madame Cartier has not been well,' and Annemarie was forced to wait and greet the new arrivals, while Raoul bore me off to the other end of the room.

'Well,' Raoul waved his arm round the room, 'what do you think of the transformation, Lucille? Unbelievable, hein?'

'Extremely attractive,' I replied. 'Monsieur Vincennes must be well off to afford all this.'

'You should see his house in Paris!' said Raoul. 'Now, that is something!' He lifted two glasses of champagne from the tray which a passing waiter proffered us, and handed me one.

'You seem to know the Vincennes very well,' I looked at him over the rim of my champagne glass.

Raoul shrugged. 'Hugo Cordet was a friend of mine. That is how I came to know the Vincennes. After his death, I kept up the acquaintanceship,' he said lightly, but even as he was speaking his eyes were straying in the direction of Annemarie as she stood welcoming the latest arrivals at her party.

Watching the practised ease with which she performed her duties, I began to feel unsure of myself again.

How could I have imagined for one single moment that I stood a chance in competition with this beautiful woman, with the luminous dark eyes, the silken jet black hair pulled severely back from the perfect oval of her face, and set in an immaculate French roll which must have taken a considerable time to achieve. Her lovely olive skin was enhanced by a form fitting dress of silver lamé, and a magnificent collar of diamonds and rubies emphasized the slender perfection of neck and shoulders.

I experienced a sharp pang of jealousy.

Annemarie Cordet seemed to have everything. Money. Time to spare. Beauty. Allure.

No wonder all the men in the ballroom kept eyeing her surreptitiously from time to time, and all the women looked slightly jaded in comparison with their hostess.

As for myself, I wished I had thought up some excuse not to come to the party. What an idiot I had been to think that mere youth could prove a match for experience and savoir faire.

I felt so disconsolate that I swallowed my champagne far too quickly, and with disastrous results. The teasing little bubbles seemed to release themselves in volume behind my nose, and I started to sneeze and splutter.

'Lucille!' said Raoul crossly. 'Don't you know better than to gulp at champagne like that!' he grabbed my glass and replaced it on the bar counter.

I sneezed again, a sneeze which brought tears to my eyes. I fumbled to open my handbag and take out a handkerchief, but the wisp of lace which I drew out was more for ornament than actual use, and it did little to blot the dampness from my cheeks and eyes.

'Here, try this,' said an amused voice behind me, and an enormous square of white cotton was thrust into my hand.

'Thanks!' I snuffled, as the recurrent bubbles kept tickling at the back of my nose. I wiped my eyes, and turned to thank the owner of the handkerchief once again, but I choked on the words, for the man who had come to my assistance was Greg MacIntosh, looking very debonair in evening suit, but with that annoyingly superior look in his eyes which I resented, relegating me as it did to the status of a silly child.

'Oh!' I muttered through clenched teeth. 'You!' And I was so fed up at once more looking like a damsel in distress in the eyes of this infuriating compatriot of mine, that I turned back to take hold of Raoul's arm and walk away from Greg, head in air, but unfortunately, Raoul was no longer standing beside me, and as I blinked away the last embarrassing champagne tears, I saw him threading his way through the guests and take up a position at Annemarie's side.

'Oh!' I repeated, more explosively. I was shaken by his desertion and stood at a loss, wondering what to do next.

'I think a walk in the garden to cool off is now on the agenda,' Greg MacIntosh firmly took my arm. 'You look almost at boiling point,' he added truthfully, but unkindly.

I tried to shake him off, but he merely strengthened his grip.

'Come on!' he urged. 'And don't flatter yourself,' he added annoyingly. 'My intentions are completely honourable!' and with that he forcefully piloted me through the laughing, gossiping groups of guests back across the ballroom to the entrance door, and out into the garden.

As we passed the place where Annemarie was standing talking to Raoul, I noticed the woman stop to watch us and her eyes narrowed with annoyance. In spite of having recaptured my Raoul, apparently she also wanted to have Greg at her beck and call, and was annoyed because one of her admirers had deserted her even for a short spell.

Greg seemed unaware of the frown directed at him, and so a little devil of wickedness inside me urged me to move closer to him and look admiringly at his handsome face, as if I genuinely enjoyed his company.

No doubt surprised by my change of attitude, Greg gave me a puzzled look, and then, aware of the other couple who were watching us, he grinned suddenly and said,

'That's the girl! I'm a great believer in not letting myself be taken for granted!'

I smiled in amusement. So Greg was being kind to me for an ulterior purpose! He was trying to make Madame Cordet jealous! Well, that put both of us in the same boat, and although I had no great fondness for his irritating company, it would suit my own book to play along with him and, giving him a conspiratorial wink, I clung even more tightly to his arm as we walked out into the garden.

It was a lovely night. There was a sharp freshness in the wind which blew down from the mountains, and it soon cooled the angry scarlet of my cheeks. In fact, it even made me shiver a little as it penetrated my thin dress, so that Greg let go of my elbow and instead, lightly circled my waist with his arm.

'It's nothing personal,' he assured me. 'It's merely that I don't want you to catch a chill, and we can hardly return to the ballroom right away now, can we? It might look as if we had quarrelled.'

As it happened, I was in no hurry to return to the villa and try and keep my end up with the brittle conversation of the smart set Annemarie had imported for her cocktail party, so I did not demur; and so, with Greg's arm warm about me, we strolled slowly down the avenue of lilacs.

High above us, the black velvet of the sky was sequinned with stars, whose incandescent light reflected off the snows of the distant High Alps with a spectral glow.

The noise of laughter and babble of high-pitched tongues could be heard from the open windows of the villa, but it seemed an alien sound which did not blend with the soft sough of the wind in the lilac plumes, or the deeper, almost hypnotic note of the fast flowing waters of the Lune as they cascaded down, in a series of waterfalls, through the deep gorge at the end of the garden to the valley below.

CHAPTER NINE

For several minutes Greg MacIntosh and I wandered in amiable silence through the scented garden. It was Greg who first spoke.

'You don't have much to say for yourself, do you?' he looked quizzically down at me.

He seemed to be criticizing my lack of conversation and I flushed self-consciously. I had let myself be entranced by the magic of the night. Annemarie would have had more sense than that.

'I was thinking,' I said defensively.

'You know,' observed MacItosh surprisingly, 'it's a pleasant change to be with a woman who doesn't prattle for the sake of hearing her own voice. Actually,' he went on as we turned to go back to the house, 'I always think that people who have to keep talking are unsure of themselves, like children who need to have a night-light burning in their nurseries, because they are afraid of the dark.'

'Grandpère says I don't speak much because I am too busy daydreaming,' I answered slowly. 'But not talking in company is not necessarily daydreaming, would you say?'

Down the garden path came the sound of approaching footsteps. From the corner of my eye, I caught a glimpse of the silver reflection of Annemarie's dress in the moonlight, and then, suddenly the glittering gown was obscured and all I could see was the star patterned heaven above me, as Greg bent over me and kissed me fully on the lips.

I was too surprised by his unexpected action to struggle, and even more surprised to find that after the first few shocked seconds I did not want to struggle.

The spell was broken when Annemarie called,

'Ah! Greg! There you are! I've been looking all over for you.'

Gently Greg released me, but before turning to answer the French girl he gave me a conspiratorial wink.

'Annemarie! I didn't hear you approach,' he lied glibly. 'I was showing Lucille how attractive your garden is by moonlight.'

'I am sure Lucille appreciated it,' said Annemarie sweetly. 'But really, Greg, don't you think she is rather young for your kind of Cook's tour?'

I flared up at her tone of condescension. Although I knew that Greg's kiss had meant nothing and that it had merely been a ruse to bring our respective partners to heel, I resented the fact that Annemarie could so lightly dismiss me as a rival, and I was trying to think up a cutting retort when Raoul Médoc, who had accompanied Annemarie into the garden, said gruffly,

'Lucille, your grandfather was wondering where you had got to. He was surprised not to find you with me!'

'Grandpère takes too much for granted at times!' I retorted, and Greg, standing behind Annemarie, gave me an appreciative grin.

'Oh! Let's get inside!' said Annemarie impatiently. 'It's far too cold to stand and talk out here,' and turning to take hold of Greg's arm with her slender hand, she started back with him towards the villa.

Raoul, whether he liked it or not, was forced to accompany me, but I dismissed him at the entrance and went over to join my grandfather, who was standing in the middle of the room surrounded by a group of old friends.

I had been chatting happily with them for about ten minutes when Annemarie, with Greg and Raoul on either arm, and followed by a crowd of her own sophisticated friends, came to join us.

Annemarie's eyes were sparkling with malice, and there was something about the way she looked at me which made me feel cold.

'Lucille!' she cried gaily as she came up to us. 'I've been hearing about you, chérie!'

Around me the chatter had stopped, and I felt uneasily that Annemarie was going to say something I didn't want to hear, but I managed to say lightly,

'I hope what you heard was to my credit!'

Annemarie giggled. She looked first at Raoul, then at Greg and her other friends.

'We—ell,' she drawled. 'Not exactly, but it was an amusing story. You shouldn't have kept it to yourself.'

Grandfather came to stand by my side, as if he sensed I was in need of support, while I looked from Raoul to Greg with a puzzled frown.

Had one or other of them said anything to Annemarie about me?

Greg avoided my gaze and Raoul looked down at his feet.

'Oh, my dear,' went on Madame Cordet, her tone mocking. 'Even at your age, you should be able to tell when a man isn't a man!'

There was a chorus of laughter from her friends.

I stood stockstill, and looked at the grinning faces in front of me. Even Raoul had started to smile, and I was furious at him for the way he had deserted me for the smart Parisienne. As for Greg, he was surveying me with an odd expression in his eyes, and a slow, hot flush of rage stained my skin from the neck upwards.

Grandfather touched my arm, as if trying to will me to keep my hot head cool, and I might have succeeded if Annemarie hadn't added spitefully.

'Yes, Lucille! I have just been told of the biggest laugh this dump has had in years! How you sent our poor Sergeant Duval on a wild goose chase along the river, because you didn't know the difference between a man and a bundle of old rags!' Her belittling tone was too much for me.

I would not, could not, let anyone, and especially a sure of herself, patronizing little socialite like Annemarie Cordet, get away with a remark like that.

I hadn't meant to say what I did, until I had proof, but say it I did.

'Dear Madame Cordet, I may not have your experience with the male sex,' I said cuttingly, 'but I can assure you I still know a real man when I see one, and especially, in this case, I can assure you it was a man I saw floating in the river, because somewhere, sometime, I have seen his face before!'

There was a collective gasp of astonishment from my audience. Even Grandfather uttered a startled exclamation as he stepped up to me, and closed his fingers so tightly round my wrist that I winced.

'What do you mean, Lucille?' he snapped.

'Exactly what I have said, Grandpère,' I retorted. 'The dead man reminded me of someone.' I puckered my lips. 'It was not the face of someone I could have identified, you understand, but rather the face of someone I felt I had met, perhaps in passing, in a café or at some social gathering – perhaps even only in the street.'

'Why did you not tell this to Sergeant Duval, or even me, to begin with?' he demanded sternly.

'What help would it have been? I mean, when I went with you to tell Duval about my dicovery, and he asked if I could identify the body, I told him the truth. I couldn't identify it! Saying that the dead man's face vaguely reminded me of someone, I knew not who, would have been no help to him at all, now would it?'

'You should still have mentioned the fact,' he said firmly.

'Well, I didn't see the necessity for it at the time,' I reiterated. 'After all, I fully expected that within a few hours at most after my report, the body would be recovered and identified by friends or relatives.' I stopped. 'It did not turn out like that at all though, but as it happened, it was as well I said nothing, Duval would only have laughed all the louder when he decided I had mistaken a turnip head for someone I had met!'

I looked round the faces which only minutes earlier had been mocking me, but whose expressions now were far from amused. 'I can tell you this,' I went on fiercely, 'I am going to make Sergeant Duval laugh on the other side of his face, even if I have to find that body again myself!'

'Lucille!' interrupted Grandfather sternly, 'you will do no such thing! You will leave a further search to the police. In fact,' he decided, 'it might be a good idea to go and have another talk with Duval right away.'

Annemarie, who had been standing looking vexed at the way I had become the centre of attraction, decided it was time the limelight shone on her once again.

'But you can't leave now, Monsieur Verlaine!' she cried, stepping forward to put an appealing hand on Grandfather's arm. 'The party is only starting! In any case,' she shrugged her pretty shoulders, 'Sergeant Duval would not exactly bless you if you confronted him with another problem tonight.' She shook her head. 'Poor man, already he has had a busy evening keeping the unusual volume of traffic to Tourloup under control, and it will be many hours yet before his task is over!'

'Annemarie is right, Monsieur Verlaine,' Raoul backed up his hostess's remarks. 'There is nothing our good sergeant could do tonight about Lucille's story. Tomorrow he will be in a much better position to look into it and organize another search of the river banks. So,' he suggested, smiling round at us, 'why spoil the party? This tragedy to an unknown touches none of us, and should not allow us to put a damper on Monsieur Vincenne's housewarming celebrations.'

'Hear, hear!' agreed the other guests.

Grandfather bowed gravely. 'You are right, Raoul. I was acting discourteously to my host. Forgive me, Monsieur Vincennes.'

The little man nodded and Raoul smiled gaily round us.

'Eh bien!' he said cheerfully. 'Let us enjoy ourselves again, eh, Lucille?' he came over to stand beside me, to Annemarie's ill-concealed chagrin, and took hold of my arm.

'Come on! You must have another glass of champagne to restore your party mood!' he pulled me gently towards the bar. 'Only this time, ma petite,' he teased, 'remember to sip the wine more slowly!'

Grandfather excused himself and rejoined his own group of friends and Annemarie, seeing that Raoul was not going to go back to her, took Greg's arm and led him off towards a party of her Riviera acquaintances.

Away from Annemarie's influence, Raoul seemed to shed the cynicism and sophistication he had acquired since he went to Paris, and which I felt had spoilt him, and reverted to his old debonair personality. We chatted happily of old friends and old times, and the mischief we had got into together as children, and between mouthfuls of the delicious savouries with which the waiters kept replenishing the plates on the bar counter, I also told him how I had finished my University examination and also about the events I had seen at the previous year's Edinburgh Festival.

It was the first time for almost two years I had enjoyed a good chat with him, and time flew happily past, so that I forgot my earlier annoyance with him for being so doting towards Annemarie and taking her side to mock me over the scarecrow incident.

We were still swapping stories of our past months' doings, when Madame Médoc came over to join us.

Raoul's mother is not exactly beautiful, but she is tall and statuesque, and what the French call a 'belle laide'. Although she subtly plays down the fact, she is a woman of strong personality and behind her facade of feminine weakness, I have sensed a will of iron and I know, from my former close contact with the family, that she, and not her husband, rules the Médoc household.

In the past, I have often felt sorry for poor Doctor Médoc. He is such a kindly, courteous little man, rather insignificant looking in appearance, with a perpetually harassed air. He obviously adores his wife and she can do what she likes with him.

Raoul is as unlike his father in every way as it is possible to be, even to the way he successfully battles his will against his mother's

I can remember how furious she was when he decided to leave Tourloup and try and make a living in his chosen profession in Paris. Grandfather said that for months after the event, she made her poor husband's life a misery and even managed to ascribe to me some of the blame for Raoul's desertion, saying, apparently, that if I had accepted Raoul when he had first proposed to me, some two years ago, he would never have dreamed of leaving Tourloup, but would have remained happily at home, carrying on his work as a free lance writer every bit as well in Tourloup as he could in Paris.

I thought Grandpapa had exaggerated this story, but I realized there must have been some truth to it, because Madame Médoc's greeting to me was short and cool, and thereafter she completely ignored me and, taking her son's arm, drew him aside.

'I have had enough of this affair,' I heard her say to him. 'And I can feel one of my attacks of migraine coming on. Since your father was too busy with some maternity case to escort me here, and since he has still failed to show up, will you please take me home? Now!' she added sharply.

Raoul hesitated.

His mother repeated her request. 'You must take me home, Raoul, this very minute!' she whispered angrily. 'My head is killing me. I cannot stand all this noise and all these stupid strangers.'

Raoul shrugged. 'Very well, Maman! I shall take you home now.' He looked across at me, 'But don't you go off with anyone else, Lucille! I shall be back as soon as possible.'

However, as it happened, before Raoul returned Grandfather decided that he, too, had had enough.

'I have a very busy day ahead of me tomorrow, Lucille,' he came over to where I was sitting alone. 'I don't like to take you away before the party is over, but I'm afraid I shall have to.'

I knew there was no use my protesting that I could wait on my own and that Raoul would be back in time to see me safely home. Grandfather, who has old-fashioned ideas to my way of thinking, would not have allowed me to do so. He had taken me to the party, therefore it was up to him to take me home.

We went to say thanks and good-bye to our host, and Monsieur Vincennes expressed his pleasure that we had been able to come, and added that he hoped to see us again soon.

'You must arrange an afternoon with Annemarie, Mademoiselle Mathieson,' he said to me. 'Then we shall show you over the rest of the villa.'

He looked round for his daughter to confirm this arrangement, but she was standing at the other side of the room with Greg MacIntosh in close attendance, as he had been ever since our romantic charade in the garden, and although I was perfectly sure she was aware that Grandfather and I were leaving, she chose to ignore her duty as hostess and, turning her back on us, she went on laughing and chattering with her circle of friends.

Grandpère and I were among the first to leave, but almost before we had reached our own gateway, we could hear the revving of engines, the sound of high pitched voices and laughter, and the roar of loud sports car exhausts, as other guests took their leave.

'Madame Cordet was right,' observed Grandfather. 'Sergeant Duval is going to have a long, busy evening ahead of him!'

He stopped at the gate and looked back along the road to

watch the twin beams of car headlights slash through the darkness, one after the other, as they went racing down the Tourloup highway.

'My only hope is that all these young people are able to control their vehicles,' he went on, shaking his head doubtfully. 'You know, that road over the Col can be tricky at night, even when you have your senses about you.'

He opened the gate.

'By the way, Lucille, tonight, when you recited that story of yours about the incident at the river, I thought about it carefully afterwards and, forgive me my dear, I began to have fresh doubts about it.'

I stopped and stared at him.

'What do you mean, Grandpère?'

'This, my child. Tell me, did you truly see a man's face and recognize it, or was your story tonight one of impulse to save your youthful pride because Madame Cordet elected to make fun of you in public?'

'Dear Grandpapa,' I said slowly, 'you have known me all my life. You know that I am quick-tempered and stubborn, and,' I sighed, 'yes, proud, but surely,' I shook my head, 'Grandpapa, surely you must have known that in a matter as serious as this, I would not make up a silly lie.'

'That's all I wanted to know, Lucille. Please forgive me for doubting you, but blame it on my legal training. I had to be very sure of my facts before arranging another appointment for you with Sergeant Duval.'

He stood aside after unlocking the front door to let me enter the house.

'And now, to bed with you, chérie, and pleasant dreams.'

He kissed me gently on the forehead.

'Good night, Grandpapa,' I returned the salute, and stifling a sleepy yawn, I went upstairs to my bedroom.

Yet, tired as I was, it was a long time before I fell asleep. I kept thinking over all the fantastic events of the day that was passing, but in spite of the mystery of a body that disappeared, the narrow escape I had had from being shot by an idiotic hunter, and the pleasing knowledge that I had been able to get Raoul away from the clutches of Annemarie Cordet's predatory little talons, my last conscious thoughts were of none of these things.

Instead, I relived again the moments in a moonlit garden, when a stranger had kissed me and I had unbelievably enjoyed the sensation, and sleepily, my hand went to my mouth to touch again the lips Greg MacIntosh had kissed, and smiling at the memory, I fell asleep.

CHAPTER TEN

It was after ten o'clock the following morning when Martha came into the bedroom to tell me it was time I was up.

She opened the long green outside shutters, and the morning sun which then came streaming through the open windows so dazzled me with its brightness, that I had to shade my eyes with my hands until they became adjusted to the brilliant light.

'You have slept well, ma petite!' Martha stood smiling down at me. 'Your grandfather told me to let you lie in, but not for too long, because you are to go and have a talk with Sergeant Duval at the police station as soon as possible.'

'Oh, dear!' I sighed sleepily. 'That puts a damper on the morning already!'

Martha chuckled. 'No doubt! I expect you had something much more interesting planned for today.' She gave me a knowing look. 'Monsieur Raoul has already been on the telephone to ask for you.'

I sat up. 'He has!' I beamed with satisfaction. 'What did I tell you, Martha? It hasn't taken him long to forget Madame Cordet, now has it?'

Martha shrugged. 'That depends. After all, he might have been telephoning about a business matter!'

'Why? Didn't he leave a message?'

'Only that he would ring back later.'

'I'll wager he wants to take me to the coast!' I said gleefully, jumping out of bed. 'It's a gorgeous day – just the very day to spend at the seaside!'

'Don't count your chickens,' warned Martha. 'Even if your friend wishes to switch his attentions, Madame Cordet is not the one who will give in easily!'

She turned to leave the room.

'Your petit déjeuner will be ready in five minutes, so don't be long.'

I had a quick shower, and after a momentary hesitation – in case Raoul wasn't going to come up to expectations – I put on a pair of rose pink denim jeans, and a shirt blouse of pink and white candy stripes. Then I brushed my hair, tied it back into a ponytail with a white nylon ribbon, and ran down to the terrace where Martha had set my breakfast.

Already the sun was so warm that, in spite of being set on cubes of ice, the pats of butter were beginning to melt.

Martha, who would never have dreamed of buying bread or cakes in a shop, makes the best croissants I have ever tasted. They are flaky, the right crispness, and have a flavour all their own. I took one, broke it into two pieces, spread it lavishly with butter, and slowly savoured the first delicious mouthful.

Ten minutes later, as I was finishing the last drop of coffee, Martha came out to tell me that Raoul Médoc had called to have a word with me.

'Show him out here to the terrace, please, Martha,' I asked, adding smugly, 'What are the odds I'll not be home for lunch today?'

She shrugged. 'We'll see,' and went off to summon Raoul.

'Bonjour, Lucille,' Raoul, looking very sleek and playboyish in dark grey trousers, white, short-sleeved, open-necked shirt with a navy silk cravat tucked neatly into the V, came striding through the open French window.

He took my outstretched hand, and with a flourish, bent to kiss it.

'You look blooming this morning, ma chérie,' he straightened up and smiled down at me. 'Late nights seem to agree with you.'

I looked up at him, but could not read the expression in his eyes because of the darkness of the glass of the sun spectacles he was wearing.

'It's my youth!' I said lightly. 'That's what does it! At my age, you can take a late night in your stride!'

'That must be the answer,' he replied amiably, sitting down on the wicker chair facing me and helping himself to the remaining croissant. 'At the moment you don't look a day over sixteen!'

'Martha told me you were on the phone for me earlier this morning,' I said, eager to know the purpose of his visit. 'Was it something important?'

'That depends on one's point of view,' he quipped, leaning back indolently in the chair.

'Yes?'

'It seems a pity, when I have only a few more days of my holiday left to waste a day like this hanging about Tourloup. I was wondering if you would like to drive down to the coast?'

I smirked to myself. So I had been right!

'I shall have to find out if Grandfather has made any other arrangements for me,' I said hesitantly, not wanting to appear too eager to accept. 'I know, for example, he wishes me to have a word with Sergeant Duval this morning.'

'About what you were speaking about last night?' asked Raoul.

I nodded.

'Surely that can wait! For one thing,' he went on, 'you would not be able to see the good Sergeant himself. I understand he has gone to Castellane to have a word with his Inspector. At least, so I heard my father say. And I don't suppose it is worth your while going to see Gaston Lebrun, who acts as stand-in.'

Raoul took another mouthful of croissant and munched it before adding,

'If I know Gaston, he will hum and haw, and finally

tell you it would be better if you saw Sergeant Duval himself.'

'You are quite sure Duval is away?' I demanded. 'It's odd Grandpapa didn't know he wouldn't be on duty.'

'It was a last minute arrangement, so Duval told my father when he saw him this morning.'

'Well!' I sighed. 'That let's me out, doesn't it? There's no good my seeing anyone but the Sergeant. I'll tell Grandfather when he comes home at lunchtime.'

'Ah! Non!' said Raoul, rising to his feet. 'You will not be here for lunch, if you come with us. We plan to leave as soon as possible.'

'We?' I queried, in surprise.

'Yes. It was Annemarie's idea that we should spend the day at the coast. She gets bored hanging about Tourloup all the time.'

'If you are going with Madame Cordet, Raoul, there is no need for me to come along too,' I said glumly, my high spirits plummetting.

'The Scots engineer fellow is coming too,' said Raoul, without enthusiasm. 'We thought we would make it a foursome.'

'Oh!' Immediately I brightened up again. 'He and Annemarie get on well together, don't they?'

'She appears to find him amusing, for the time being,' said Raoul lightly. 'I can't understand it, but then, it is not my concern, is it, Lucille?' He leaned forward and took my hand in his. 'You are the one who interests me!'

I let him hold my fingers for a few seconds before gently pulling away from him.

'If you don't mind waiting until I telephone Grandpapa,' I excused myself, 'I shall see if it is all right for me to go with you.'

Raoul took a cigarette from a slim gold case and lit it with a matching gold lighter, as I stood up to go to the telephone.

'I shan't be minutes,' I assured him, and hurried off.

Grandfather agreed with me there was no point in going to the gendarmerie if Sergeant Duval wasn't on duty.

'When he returns tomorrow, we shall go and see him together, you would prefer that, wouldn't you?'

I agreed, adding, 'And is it all right to go down to Cannes with Raoul and Madame Cordet?' I asked. 'Or did you have something else arranged for me?'

'No, child. Off you go and enjoy yourself, but remember,' he chuckled, 'no arguments with Madame Cordet, or I can see more sparks flying!'

'I'll be very good, Grandpère,' I assured him. 'I'll not even make eyes at Greg MacIntosh once to upset her.'

We wished each other 'Au revoir' and hung up, and I went back out to the terrace to tell Raoul I would be delighted to make up the party.

'Whose car will we be going in?' I asked. 'Mine is still with Jacques at the garage.'

'MacIntosh insists on driving his own,' said Raoul. 'Annemarie will be travelling with him. However,' he stubbed out his cigarette, 'you and I will go together in my car.'

'Good!' I said with relief. At least, during the time it took to drive to the coast and back, I would not be in Annemarie's condescending company, and therefore more likely to follow my grandfather's advice.

'Are you ready, then, Lucille?' Raoul stood up and moved towards the French window.

'Give me a couple of minutes to get my swim suit and beach accessories and I'll be right with you!' I smiled at him gaily. 'Oh! And I must remember my sun glasses.'

I surveyed him critically. 'Where did you buy the spectacles you are wearing, Raoul?' I asked. 'I have never been able to get ones with such smoky dark glass, or such an attractive shape. They give you a lovely sinister air.'

I giggled. 'Do you think an air of mystery would go well with my ponytail?'

'Ma chère!' Raoul gave an exaggerated bow. 'You would look mysterious and exciting in anything!'

I chuckled at his grand manner and ran off into the house, up the stairs to my bedroom two at a time, grabbed the beachbag which I had hopefully filled and laid out in readiness, and humming to myself, I dashed downstairs again and into the kitchen to inform Martha I would not be home for lunch, and also that I had been right, and she had been wrong about the reason for Raoul's telephone call and visit.

Raoul had gone out to wait for me in his car and as I came out to join him, I paused for a moment to give it an admiring look.

The funny, elderly little Citroën which had once been Raoul's pride had been deposed by a handsome red Mercedes, and I couldn't help thinking how well Raoul must be doing in Paris to afford such a luxury model. It said a lot for him, at only twenty-three, to be earning this kind of money in a highly competitive field, and I felt rather proud of him as I got into the seat beside him and fastened my safety belt.

'Annemarie and MacIntosh are waiting for us at the garage,' Raoul told me as we drove down the High Street. 'Look, there they are;' he indicated Greg's white Alfa Romeo, which was standing in the forecourt.

Raoul tooted his horn as he accelerated past the garage.

'We shall be at Cannes long before they will!' he laughed as I turned to wave to the occupants of the other car. 'In fact, I'll bet you I'll have downed a couple of Camparis before they join us at the Carlton.'

'The Carlton!' I raised my brows. 'We've never gone there before,' and I wondered if the choice of rendezvous was Raoul's to impress Annemarie, or if Annemarie herself had chosen the spot.

As we left Tourloup behind, I was very glad I had taken the trouble to fasten the car safety belt round me. In his old, small powered Citroën, Raoul had never been able to go very fast, and consequently I had not realized what a speed fiend he was.

Unfortunately, his driving know-how at speed was not all it should have been, and after the first ten minutes on the switchback Col road, with its vicious bends taken as even a novice should have known not to take them, I felt sick, both with fear that we should never arrive at our destination in one piece and physically from the way we swayed and braked sharply on the corners.

'I told you we should be in Cannes first!' said Raoul, glancing at his watch when we reached the main road to the coast. 'That's my fastest time from Tourloup to the junction yet!'

Because the road we were joining was a 'route protegée', he had to halt at the junction to wait for a gap in the stream of traffic racing south, but I had the uneasy feeling that if it hadn't been for the presence of the motor-cycle traffic police team on the other side of the road, blandly waiting for someone to infringe the rule of the road, he would have risked filtering into the main road without stopping.

As it was, he sat drumming his fingers impatiently on the steering wheel, until I said in exasperation,

'Honestly Raoul, getting to Cannes is not a matter of life or death. What does a few minutes' delay matter?'

'I want to win a bet with Annemarie,' he said sulkily. 'Now it looks as if I might not,' and he glared in his driving mirror as MacIntosh's Alfa pulled smoothly in at our back.

As it happened, Raoul was able to get away during a brief lull, but Greg was left behind and so we did arrive first at the Carlton, and Raoul jubilantly downed a couple of Camparis in rapid succession before Annemarie and Greg MacIntosh put in an appearance.

Greg, in a plaid shirt and dark grey-green trousers looked almost touristy beside Raoul's casual elegance, but his companion made up for him.

Annemarie looked the height of sophistication in very tight, black satinized-linen slacks and a black halter-neck blouse. She had black-framed, domino-shaped sunglasses, which gave her an almost Mephistophelean look, and every bit of her hair was hidden under a scarlet silk scarf, tied pirate-wise at the back of her neck, and a round, gold gipsy ear-ring dangled from one ear.

Everyone in the cocktail bar turned to look at her as she came in, because even in this centre of sophistication she was outstanding.

'I told you we should get here first!' Raoul raised his third glass of Campari in salute. 'And if we had not been held up at the road junction, there would have been a quarter of an hour in it!'

Annemarie perched herself up on a bar stool.

'If Greg had let me drive, you would never have won your bet,' she said sulkily. 'He simply would not put his foot down on the corners!'

'Greg is a real canny Scot!' I spoke in English, and I involuntarily gave him a sympathetic smile. 'I don't think I would have put my foot down on the corners either!'

'Didn't you enjoy your drive down?' Raoul looked at me in surprise.

'I expect it is because, like most drivers, I prefer driving to being driven,' I replied tactfully. 'I'm not used to a chauffeur.'

'What are you drinking?' Greg MacIntosh sat down between me and Annemarie.

'I'd like another orange pressé, with lots of ice, thanks.'

'I see you are still playing the part of the ingénue,' sneered Annemarie. 'Thank goodness, I have grown up,' she switched her gaze to Greg. 'I'll have, let me see,' she pouted prettily, 'oh dear, I can't make up my mind. Raoul,' she smiled beyond me to where Médoc was seated, 'you know my tastes, chérie. You choose – something with oomph!'

'How about an Alexander?' suggested Raoul.

'Un Alexandre? Ah! Oui! Un Alexandre, please, Greg, and another Campari for Raoul – that's right, isn't it?'

It was obvious that Annemarie was trying to show me how very friendly she and Raoul were, but I refused to let her rile me.

Greg signalled the barman and gave the order, choosing a light ale for himself.

'I'm famished!' said Annemarie when she had finished her drink. 'Let's eat before the place gets too busy. Raoul!' she went on imperiously, 'see if you can get hold of a menu while we have another apéritif.'

In spite of my good resolutions I felt my hackles rise at the way she was trying to appropriate Raoul and make me feel out of it, but I counted to ten once, twice, three times, and managed to swallow my temper.

Surely Raoul wouldn't let himself be bossed about like this! I told myself, and I willed him to disobey her.

To my astonishment, it was Greg who stepped out of line.

'Must we eat here?' he demanded. 'I know of a small place a mile or two further along the coast, where the food is superb, and which has a private foreshore which is not only sandy, but uncrowded! I suggest we go there.'

'Is it that you cannot afford the prices here, Greg?' asked Annemarie tactlessly. 'Do not worry. Today, I shall be the hostess!'

Greg looked so taken aback by this suggestion, I almost laughed aloud, but my amusement changed to apprehension when I saw twin white spots appear under the taut skin of his flaring nostrils – a danger signal if ever I saw one.

Before his wrath could explode, I interpolated hastily,

'I didn't expect to come to a place like this myself,' I smiled shyly round. 'I don't feel dressed for dining here. Raoul,' I put my fingers on his bare forearm, 'these big fashionable places overwhelm me. Couldn't we go on to one of our usual old haunts – Chez Cassime's or the Moulin Jaune? Something like that?'

As I spoke, I heard Greg MacIntosh softly expel a long, slow breath and the tightness disappeared from his face.

'You would like Chez Martine, then, Lucille. And you will, too, Annemarie,' he added, hastily turning to the pretty widow. 'As a Parisienne you will be interested to know that the chef of Chez Martine started his training at Laserre's, and if you like the dishes served in the Paris house, you will certainly appreciate the menu there.'

For perhaps a minute Greg and Annemarie eyed each other with the determination of people who are used to getting their own way, but in the end, it was Annemarie who gave in.

'Very well then,' she shrugged her shoulders gracefully and slipped off the bar seat. 'Chez Martine's it shall be, Greg, if that is all right with you two?' she added as an afterthought.

'If that's what you wish,' agreed Raoul, and I nodded, making my ponytail bounce up and down on the nape of my neck.

'I'll lead the way,' said Greg decisively, and took Annemarie's arm.

Raoul and I followed them out of the Carlton to the car park, where I noticed that Greg, as if to placate Annemarie for going against her wishes in the choice of eating places, showed her into the driving seat and let her take the wheel of his precious Alfa for the next part of the ride.

CHAPTER ELEVEN

The meal at Chez Martine was every bit as good as Greg had promised, and even the sophisticated Madame Cordet declared she had never tasted such an excellent Gourmandise Brillat Savarin, and Raoul concurred.

When we left the dining-room, we were too replete with food to do other than walk down the long flight of steps, cut from the rock face itself, which led to a little sandy cove at the foot of the cliffs, and here we looked for a suitable place to laze and sunbathe.

Since my fair skin does not take kindly to too much exposure to the southern sun until it has become acclimatized, I found a suitably shaded place for myself between two high boulders, and sat down.

Annemarie, on the other hand, with her olive skin, did not run the same risk of burning, so she spread her gaudy bathing towel on the sandy beach and made use of the rocky enclosure as a dressing-room to change from her striking black outfit into the briefest of white bikinis.

Then she covered her head with a white straw sun hat and went sauntering back along the beach to lie down on her towel. By this time, both Greg and Raoul had also changed to bathing trunks. In comparison with Greg's rather square figure, the Frenchman looked slim and supple as a ballet dancer, yet the contrast, while it emphasized their difference in physiques, was not altogether to Greg's disadvantage.

'Raoul!' called Annemarie imperiously as they walked towards her. 'My sun oil is over there' – she indicated her beachbag which lay a mere couple of yards beyond her own reach – 'would you be an angel and oil my back for me – but be most careful of my costume – the oil might stain it.'

So saying, she lay prone on the ground, cradling her head on her arms to wait for her command to be carried out, and never doubting for a moment that Raoul would not do as he had been bid.

'Oh, and Greg,' she murmured, turning her face to the young engineer, 'would you be a pet and light a cigarette for me?'

Again I had to chalk up a good mark for MacIntosh, because instead of eagerly carrying out her order, from where he was squatting on the sand he lazily tossed her his box of cigarettes and matches, and then he stretched himself and lay supine on the coarse sand to enjoy the feel of the sun on his chest.

For a long time, no one spoke. We were all content to lie and drowse in the warmth and sunshine, and the only sounds to break the stillness were the soft lapping of the waves against the shingle and the distant hum of traffic from the roadway high above us.

At length I tired of idleness, changed to my swimsuit and wandered down to the edge of the water.

I had barely put my toes in its delicious coolness, when Greg got up and came down to join me.

'You shouldn't go in swimming so soon after a meal,' he advised.

'Old maid!' I grimaced. 'In any case, it must be well over an hour since we dined. We've been dozing for ages!' and with that I waded out and plunged breathlessly into the sea.

Greg followed and was soon alongside.

'Do you do any skin diving?' he asked, as we swam slowly

towards the wooden raft which the owners of Chez Martine had anchored in the little cove.

'No,' I replied. 'But I should love to try.'

'Perhaps next week, when I have another day off, you could come and join a group of my friends who are keen. You will be able to borrow some equipment from them.'

He clambered aboard the raft, but had no sooner done so than Annemarie and Raoul pulled themselves aboard too.

I wore no bathing cap, but Madame Cordet had on a fabulous creation of multi-coloured rubber flowers which danced and shimmered each time she moved her head.

'Come, Greg,' she challenged, 'I shall race you back to the shore.'

'Let me get my breath back first,' he replied lazily.

Annemarie stood up and prodded him with her scarlet-nailed toes.

'Come on!' she said impatiently.

'MacIntosh is afraid you will leave him behind in the water, as I did on the land!' goaded Raoul.

'And I am afraid that my skin will frizzle if I stay here any longer!' I, too, stood up, suddenly aware of the prickle of heat across my sea wet shoulders, and I dived back into the water and made for the shore.

No one made any attempt to accompany me, and I was back on shore, drying myself off in the shade of my rocky enclosure, when my companions eventually decided to leave the raft.

I stood watching them as they came racing for the shore, thinking there was little to choose between the standard of their strokes. They all seemed to reach the water's edge at the same instant, but Annemarie, glowing with elation, insisted that she had won and the men good-humouredly agreed, as they came running up the sands towards me.

'You should have waited, Lucille,' called Annemarie. 'Then we could all have had a race.'

'I'm afraid I am not in your class,' I replied truthfully, but sadly, thinking that here was one more sphere in which Annemarie was superior to me.

I changed back into my pink denim jeans and candy striped blouse, but Annemarie, apart from taking off her exotic bathing cap and replacing it with the shady sun hat, did not bother to change, but lay down in her damply clinging bikini for another session of sunbathing.

'I must go back to my car for my camera,' Raoul said, looking down at her.

'Don't be silly, Raoul! It is far too hot to climb up all these steps for such a trifle. Moreover, you have already taken dozens of pictures of me this week.' She shot me a malicious look.

I turned away to hide my vexation. Raoul was supposed to be my friend, so she had no right to flaunt her own intimacy with him in my face.

I willed Raoul to say something which would show his resumed interest in me, but instead, before going for his camera, he teasingly trickled sand through his fingers on to Annemarie's back, and I realized, bleakly, that he had forgotten about me. Madame Cordet had only had to give him an extra flutter with her long eyelashes, and he was back under her spell.

Well, I could hardly blame him, I thought despondently. Annemarie was beautiful, provocative, and gay, and moreover, I had told him often enough in the past that I would never take his attentions seriously. I couldn't have it both ways, could I?

On the other hand, it was most unfair that on an outing like this, Annemarie couldn't be satisfied with the man who had brought her. She had Greg MacIntosh dancing attendance on her, so why did she have to want Raoul too?

I turned my back on them and busied myself combing out the tangles in my wet hair, and letting it hang loose and limp over my shoulders.

'You look like a little girl lost!'

I hadn't heard Greg come up behind me, and I turned round with a start.

'Oh, go away!' I said angrily. 'I don't know why I ever let myself be talked into coming here today.'

Greg grinned impishly. 'I don't see anyone talking you into doing anything you don't want to do, Lucille,' he looked down at me. 'Your trouble was that you did not appreciate the strength of the opposition!' and with this encouraging remark he turned and sauntered back to Annemarie's side.

I sat on among the rocks, glowering out at them, and watching for Raoul's return. When he did come back, I assured myself, I would see to it that he remembered whom he had asked on this outing!

Actually, Greg MacIntosh made this easy for me, for he challenged Annemarie to another race, and they were swimming together far out at the point of the cove when Raoul returned.

'Where on earth has Annemarie got to?' he demanded, when he saw the empty beach.

I pointed to where the two heads bobbed up and down, very close together in the water.

Raoul stared out across the cove with such an expression of vexation on his face that I could not help feeling sorry for him. What if he was genuinely attracted to the flirtatious Parisienne? What if he was presuming on our old friendship to try and make her jealous? After all, from what I had gathered from Martha, Raoul had been very close to Annemarie for a number of months, and it seemed to me that any friendship with Madame Cordet which withstood the test of time must be genuine, for to my way of thinking she was such a self-centred, vain young woman, she would bore most people to death after a short acquaintanceship!

I studied Raoul's face. He looked tense and nervous, and this opinion was confirmed by the way he ground out a cigarette he had lit only seconds earlier, and selected another.

Poor soul, he *was* in a bad way, and it was a shame for Annemarie to lead him on as she did, I thought, quite forgetting how I myself had flirted with him in the past!

'Raoul!' I said softly. 'You shouldn't let Annemarie see how much you care for her. She's only playing with you. It isn't even as if anything could come of the affair. For one thing, you are so much younger than she is – at least six years

– and for another, you don't belong to her world. However good your present job is, you couldn't afford to keep up with her!'

'But we do belong to the same world!' cried Raoul emphatically. 'We do!' His eyes flashed. 'I intend to marry her, Lucille! She is all that a woman should be. She leads the kind of life I have always wanted to lead!' He fixed me with a strange blank stare. 'She will be mine, and not you nor anyone else will stop me!'

I shook my head in pity.

'Raoul, you idiot,' I said. 'Can't you see she is only amusing herself with you? You make a diverting companion for her here in Tourloup; you are someone useful to have at her beck and call, but believe me, if Madame Cordet marries again, it will be to someone of her own kind, with plenty of money, and plenty of time to spare for her, not someone who earns what to her must be a mere pittance, and who would have to leave her to go about his daily business.'

'You don't know what you are talking about, Lucille!' he retorted. 'But how could you?' his glance pitied me. 'In spite of your French blood, you are as frigid as all Anglo-Saxon women! There is not an ounce of passion in you.'

'Oh!' I said furiously. 'Well, let me tell you, Raoul Médoc, I should much rather be the way I am, than lure on every man I meet with false promises! What is more' – I stopped for breath – 'if you think a woman like Annemarie Cordet would give up her way of living to put up with the disorganization of a journalist's life, and his salary, and all for love, you must be completely out of your mind.'

Raoul gave me a long, slow, deliberate look, and then said in a peculiar tone, 'And to think I was feeling sorry for you! Thank goodness I am not a sentimentalist!'

'Why should you feel sorry for me?' I said crossly. 'I can look after myself!'

Raoul smiled, a malevolent smile which made me feel uncomfortable.

'I shouldn't be too sure of that!' he sneered, and with that he strode away from me, down to the water's edge, where

Annemarie was emerging from the sea a yard or two ahead of Greg.

I watched him go, and was amazed that with his going, I experienced a feeling not of anger at his dereliction, but of relief that the affair was finally over.

I wasn't cut out for this battle of the sexes. Annemarie could have Raoul, and welcome! Over the years since childhood I had felt myself grow imperceptibly less fond of him. His personal ambitions and the type of life he wanted to lead did not altogether appeal to me, but I had clung to him as some women cling to their first dance programme, or their first Valentine, for sentimental reasons. Now, all that was over, and I had no regrets at all! I felt almost light-headed!

For the next half-hour, I lay contentedly on my beach towel, enjoying the peace of mind I had achieved, and idly playing with the sand by my side, while Raoul took innumerable snaps of his beloved Annemarie in the water; Annemarie with her swimming cap on; with it off; lying supine on the sand, lying prone on the sand; Annemarie, in fact, in every possible pose, and Annemarie never tired! She enjoyed every minute, continually sending me sly little glances every now and then to see how I was reacting.

Greg MacIntosh, who had changed from his swimming trunks back to his slacks and plaid shirt, sat beside me and watched their antics.

Once, when they had gone to the water's edge and were out of earshot, he said,

'What's happened with Raoul, Lucille? A lovers' quarrel?'

I laughed. 'You could call it that!' I said lightly. I saw no reason to let Greg MacIntosh know the truth of what had happened between Raoul and me, so I added, 'but it's nothing to worry about.'

At last Raoul's spool gave out, and Annemarie decided it was time for her to change from her bikini.

When she was dressed, she gave Raoul her beachbag to carry, saying tauntingly to Greg,

'This time it is Raoul's turn to drive me home! You are

too much of a slow-coach!' and with that she took Raoul's free arm and sauntered off with him.

I stifled a sigh of relief. After my quarrel with Raoul, I hadn't been looking forward to the drive back to Tourloup with him.

Greg, however, naturally looked taken aback at the new arrangement, but since I raised no objections, there was nothing he could do.

Raoul and Annemarie left first in the scarlet Mercedes and it was obvious from the way he started off that Raoul was determined to set up a new record time for the return trip.

This made me gladder than ever about the change of partners, and I almost felt sorry for Annemarie having to suffer his erratic speeding.

It was several minutes before Greg and I could follow them, because someone in the hotel had parked his car at an angle in front of us, boxing us in, and Greg had to ask the hotel manager to find the owner and ask him to move his car.

By the time we left, the Mercedes had disappeared from sight round the point where the dirt road leading to the hotel joined the main coast road.

Greg's driving was as unlike Raoul's as the two men were in every other aspect of character and appearance. There was nothing showy or fanciful or devil-may-care about the way he handled his car, but I have rarely sat beside a smoother or more able driver, and after the first minutes I was able to relax and sit back and enjoy the ride.

As if aware of my loss of tension, Greg gave me a quick sideways glance.

'Everything all right?'

'With me? Yes! I was rather dreading going back with Raoul. He fancies himself as a speed king, but he gets there more by luck than skill.'

'Luck doesn't always hold,' said Greg gravely. 'I hope he gets Annemarie home safely.'

I didn't want to talk about either Raoul or Annemarie. I

felt I'd had enough of them for one day, so I changed the subject.

'Greg, how long will you be staying in Tourloup?' I asked him.

He shook his head. 'I'm not sure.'

'Have you decided whether this new road is a worthwhile proposition or not?'

'I've still some survey work to do before any decision is made. A lot depends on the amount of rubble blocking the old rail line.'

For another few miles we drove without speaking, and like the silence between us in the lilac garden on the previous evening, it was a friendly rather than an awkward silence.

'Daydreaming again?' quizzed Greg as we turned off the main north-south road on to the minor road which led over the Col de la Lune.

'Thinking!' I contradicted, with a smile.

Our speed slackened as we approached the highest part of the road, which had been blasted out of the rock of the mountain, and which clung precariously to the hillside with a great precipitous wall looming over it.

Soon we were over the top and approaching the parking bay where I had stopped my Rapier – could it only have been two days ago?

'It was down there I found the body,' I said, pointing to the track which led down to the water meadow. 'I wish I had never stopped!'

'You really are worried about what you saw aren't you, Lucille?'

'I keep thinking how awful it would be if the body I saw, and which Duval failed to recover, happened to be found by some of the children who play along the lower banks of the Lune.' I shivered. 'It was bad enough for me,' I was going to add, but the words were never uttered.

Greg uttered a cry of warning and simultaneously changed down and pressed hard on the accelerator, sending the car shooting forward.

His presence of mind and fantastically quick reaction

saved us from being bowled off the road and over the hundred foot drop to the gorge below. As it was, the rear bumper was grazed by an enormous boulder which had come hurtling down from the precipice above us, on to the roadway from which it rebounded and went crashing noisily down into the deep, shadowy valley below.

CHAPTER TWELVE

Greg MacIntosh slowed the car with a series of jabs on the foot brake.

'You appear to be accident prone, Lucille,' he observed, tightly. 'Three narrow escapes from death in as many days must be a record!'

'Well, they do say, don't they, that everything goes in threes!'

With an effort I kept my voice steady, although my heart was thumping painfully against my ribs, and my lips had that uncomfortable, prickly pins and needles feeling they get when shock or excitement has drained the blood from them.

'It should be all right from now on!' I added.

Greg steered the car into a parking bay at the side of the road, stopped the car and turned to look at me approvingly.

'You know, you are quite a girl, Lucille Mathieson,' he said quietly. 'There are very few people who could take a narrow escape like that in their stride.'

'You didn't react too badly yourself,' I said lightly, glad that MacIntosh could not be aware how my bones felt like jelly.

Greg laughed, and said teasingly.

'Of course, I've had a bit of recent practice on how to evade trouble on the Col de la Lune!'

I smiled back at his banter, and my tension relaxed.

Greg was a good man to be with in a tight corner, I decided. Far too good a man, my instinct told me, to be involved with a flibbertigibbet like Annemarie Cordet. Of course, his admiration for her might be the well known attraction of opposites for each other, and if so, I felt sorry for him.

'I think I'll walk back along the road,' Greg interrupted my thoughts. 'It would be a good idea to see that the road hasn't been made unsafe for traffic, because any blockage on that particular corner could prove fatal to the unwary.'

He switched off the ignition.

'You wait here and have a cigarette until I come back.'

'I don't smoke, Greg,' I said, feeling a bit peeved because he hadn't noticed this fact. 'In any case, I'd rather come along with you than stay here on my own.' I glanced round me. 'I don't know what it is, but today,' I shivered, 'this place gives me the creeps.'

Greg gave me a searching look. 'I don't blame you for feeling nervous,' he placed a warm hand over mine. 'So, if you'd rather, come with me by all means.'

It took us several minutes to walk back to the spot where the boulder had crashed down, and when we reached it, we discovered that the impact of the massive stone had made an appreciable hole in the road with cracks radiating out from it in every direction.

'Thank goodness, we were lucky enough to dodge that little lot!' Greg's mouth tightened grimly. 'There wouldn't have been much chance of coming out from under it alive.'

He glanced critically from the roadway up the length of the overhanging cliff.

'I don't see where a boulder that size could have come from,' he frowned. 'The rock face appears quite smooth right to the top. Even there, judging from the geological formation, it must slope off away from the road.'

'What does it matter?' I said quickly, having no desire to hang around the danger spot any longer than was necessary. 'It fell and that's that.'

Greg continued to look puzzled. 'But it shouldn't have, if my reading of the ground is correct.'

'For goodness sake!' I said irritably. 'You don't imagine

someone deliberately pushed it over!' I shook my head. 'Greg, you don't know this road. It is always having minor landslides. That's why those 'chute de pierres' notices are stuck in all over the place.'

'I can understand slides at other parts of the road, where there is a lot of loose scree, but at this point,' he shook his head stubbornly, 'it doesn't make sense.'

'Those huge erratic boulders are strewn all over the top of the precipice. If you go up there some time you will see them. This one could have been nearer the edge than most, and possibly undermined by the recent heavy rain they've had here.'

'I suppose that's the explanation,' Greg muttered, pushing aside a jagged portion of the boulder which had been broken from the main mass when it struck the ground. 'I think I'll get in touch with the local roadworks when I get back and tell them to check up on the situation before there is a serious accident. We happened to be lucky, others might not.'

He kicked aside some smaller pieces of rock which were strewn across the roadway.

'That should do for the meantime,' he decided, looking about him.

I wandered to the edge of the road and looked down at the trail of devastation which the boulder had caused during its hurtling descent to the river bed.

The whole rock face was scarred, out-jutting ledges had been knocked off, shrubs torn out by the roots, and even the sturdy branches of a pine which grew at right angles to the precipice had been broken away.

Somehow the sight of this strip of destruction affected me more deeply than the damage to the road surface, or perhaps it was merely delayed shock, but all of a sudden I started to tremble uncontrollably. My very flesh quivered, my teeth rattled like loose marbles in a box, and I felt deathly cold.

'Lucille!' exclaimed Greg, and came swiftly to my side. 'Lucille!'

He took me in his arms and held me tightly against his

strong body, pressing my head with his hand against the soft wool front of his shirt.

'Lucille!' he said softly for the third time. 'You poor child!'

Gently he stroked my hair as I clung to him, glad of the feel of his comforting arm about me; glad to be able to bury my face away from the sight of that trail so savagely blazed by the falling boulder; glad that I had not been alone in my own car when the landslide had occurred.

After a moment or two, the warmth from Greg's body thawed out the ice of fear which had frozen my bloodstream, and gradually I stopped trembling, but I made no effort to release myself from MacIntosh's embrace. I felt so safe in his arms, and after what I had been through, it was a wonderful feeling.

It was the horn of an approaching car which brought me back to reality, and I gently pushed myself free.

'I'm sorry for making such an idiot of myself,' I apologized shamefacedly. 'I don't know what came over me.' I stepped away from him and tried to smooth my dishevelled hair with my fingers.

'My dear child,' said Greg kindly, 'your behaviour was perfectly natural. I expect you will feel much better now that you have got the shock out of your system like that.'

He sounded so paternal I couldn't help saying,

'Yes, Father!' and my cheeks dimpled perkily.

'Brat!' Greg gave a relieved laugh. 'It's nice to have you back to normal!' and he retaliated to my remark by giving me a smart smack on the bottom.

'Come on, lass. We had better get a move on now, or your Raoul and Annemarie will be wondering what we are up to!'

'My Raoul!' I sniffed. What would Greg say if I told him that the possessive adjective no longer applied? That I had had my final quarrel with my former boyfriend, and the truth was I couldn't care less if I never saw him again!

It was on the tip of my tongue to tell him all this, but I changed my mind. After all, what did Greg care if I had finished with Raoul?

We went back to the car and Greg drove along at a sedate pace, keeping an eye well open for every possible hazard.

I opened my bag and took out a comb to try and smooth my tangled hair, and when I got it into a neat ponytail once more, I put away the comb and set about repairing my make-up, and especially adding extra colour to my lips from which I had earlier nervously licked away all traces of lipstick.

'How long do you usually spend in Tourloup when you come to visit your grandfather?' Greg asked conversationally.

'Since my parents' deaths, I have spent all my holidays here, and in summer that has meant from June until College recommenced in October,' I told him. 'This year, however, I expect it won't be quite the same.'

'How is that? Have you finished your degree course?'

I nodded. 'Yes, I am flying back to Edinburgh next week for the graduation ceremony. Then I shall return here until I can make up my mind whether to enter a teachers' training college or take a short secretarial course in London.'

'What does Monsieur Verlaine advise you to take up?'

'Grandpapa?' I smiled. 'He's quite out of date! He would like me to stay on here with him, as a lady of leisure, until I get married! You see, he is not a believer in careers for women.'

'Well, it does seem rather a waste to continue training for a career, if you have no intention of making use of that training.'

'You sound exactly like Grandpapa!' I shook my head. 'But Greg, no training is ever wasted! And tell me – what could I do with myself here? I mean to say, Martha would never let me cook a thing in her precious kitchen, or let me help about the house. She would say it wasn't "convenable" or some such nonsense. And I can't very well fill in time by arranging flowers from morning to night.'

'Annemarie seems to find plenty to occupy herself with,' said Greg blandly.

'Running from one cocktail party to the next, or one mannequin parade to the next, is not exactly my idea of occupying myself!' I said sourly.

We had reached Tourloup and Greg slowed down as we entered the cobbled High Street.

'I expect the other two will be waiting for us at the Villa des Lilas,' supposed Greg, and his supposition proved correct when we spotted the red Mercedes parked outside the gates of Annemarie's house.

'What on earth have you two been up to?' asked Annemarie suspiciously as we stopped alongside. 'Raoul and I arrived back here hours ago!'

'You said yourself that I was a slow driver,' replied Greg guilelessly, 'and it always takes much longer climbing the hills to Tourloup than it does going downhill to the coast.'

'Even so, you must have crawled back!' said Annemarie in disgust. 'It must have been deadly dull. Thank goodness, I came with Raoul,' she gave me a sly look.

'Raoul came over the pass like a racing driver. I've never enjoyed the run so much!'

Raoul preened himself, as Annemarie went on,

'Even if I had to pay out again, it was worth it!' she sighed. 'It's funny though, how I am never lucky when it comes to gambling.'

'Perhaps it's because you are so lucky in love,' I replied sweetly.

Raoul gave me a nasty look, and Greg hastily intervened.

'It was just as well you didn't come with me, Annemarie,' he said quietly. 'As it happens, Lucille and I escaped a very nasty accident only by a hair's breadth.'

'I wonder if it was the same idiot?' said Raoul. 'Someone came round a hairpin right in the middle of the road, and I thought we had had it!'

'Actually, chéri, in that instance, you were the idiot, because you were far too far over the yellow line, but n'importe,' shrugged Annemarie. 'No one was hurt.'

'In our case, it wasn't careless driving, but a rock fall which almost had us over the side,' said Greg. 'If it had happened seconds earlier, we wouldn't be here to tell the tale!'

'Well, you did escape, so why worry about it now?' said Annemarie, taking out her compact and dusting her nose with powder. 'We have been absolutely roasted sitting here in the car waiting for you.' She put away the compact. 'What I could do with right now is a long, cool drink, so how about all coming up to the house for one?'

'If you don't mind, count me out, please,' I said, feeling I had had enough of her charm for the day.

'It's all right, mon enfant,' she smiled sweetly. 'There are loads of fresh oranges for your favourite drink!'

'I am sure there are,' I replied, equally sweetly, 'but I didn't mean to be away so long, and Grandfather may be worrying about me.'

'Greg! You will come, won't you?' she invited in her husky voice.

'I'll take Lucille home first,' he replied.

'You needn't trouble,' I said crisply, and I pushed open the car door and got out before he could argue. 'I meant to ask you to drop me off at Jacques' garage as it was, so that I could find out if my own car is ready yet.'

'Are you quite sure?' asked Greg politely.

'Quite!' I nodded my head vigorously as I slammed the door shut. 'Thanks for the drive home, and everything.'

Greg started to say something in reply, but his words were lost in the noise of the engine of Raoul's car as he started it up, and without once looking in my direction, went racing through the gateway and up the drive of the Villa des Lilas.

With a casual wave, Greg followed, and I was left standing alone in the roadway, somewhat ruefully gazing after them.

CHAPTER THIRTEEN

The Rapier was not quite ready when I called at Jacques' garage.

'André has still to make sure the lighting system is in order, and I should like to take it out on the road for ten minutes, to check the brakes and steering,' Jacques informed me. 'We should not be very long.'

'Good!' I nodded. 'In that case, I shall pop into your office and have a chat with Thérèse until you are ready.'

'I didn't expect you back from Cannes so early,' went on Jacques, 'otherwise I should have had the car waiting for you. Did you have a nice day?'

'Comme-ci, comme-ça,' I shrugged, not wanting to be reminded of an afternoon when I had had the unusual experience of being the odd woman out.

Jacques grinned.

'I must say I felt sorry for you when I realized you were to be Raoul's passenger. For someone who is used to driving, to be in a car driven by that one must be torture!'

He followed me into the office, still talking.

'Our Raoul seems to fancy himself as a second Tino Makinnen, although he hasn't a clue about how to handle a car properly. I am surprised he hasn't had a major accident to date.'

'I was certainly glad to get to Cannes in one piece,' I admitted frankly. 'As you say, poor Raoul is not much of a driver. It's heel to toe on brake and accelerator, usually at the wrong times too!'

'Poor Raoul be damned!' snorted Jacques. 'He thinks he is being clever, and he won't listen to those who know. He is just a great big show off!'

'Don't listen to my brother, Lucille!' smiled Thérèse, getting up from behind her desk and coming forward to shake hands with me. 'He is only jealous because Raoul managed to get away from Tourloup and live in Paris.'

'Who wants to live in Paris?' retorted Jacques. 'Why, it isn't worthwhile having a car there for all the traffic and the parking restrictions. No! Give me Tourloup any day and especially once this new road gets built! Then there will be no need to go to a city to become rich!'

Jacques rolled a cigarette for himself.

'Yes,' he went on, 'the sooner they begin work on the new highway, the happier I shall be.'

André tapped at the office door.

'Everything is in order now, Jacques, if you want to take the Rapier for a road test.'

'Good!' Jacques nodded to him. 'I'll not be long, Lucille.'

'Don't hurry back,' said Thérèse. 'I want to hear all about the party last night at the Villa des Lilas. Tell me, Lucille, is it true that they have transformed the cellars into a fabulous ballroom?'

For the next quarter of an hour, I told Thérèse about the party, about the villa, and about the guests who had attended the house-warming.

'I'll bet Madame Cordet looked a dream!' sighed Thérèse. 'She always has the most gorgeous clothes! It must be nice to have a rich father.'

'Or to be a wealthy widow!' I said dryly.

Thérèse looked at me in surprise.

'Madame Cordet is not a wealthy widow. Far from it!'

'I thought Raoul said her husband was the director of a big plastics factory.'

'That was so, Lucille, but apparently Cordet lived up to his income and beyond it! He and his wife went through money like water, and when he died, as the result of an automobile accident, there wasn't a penny piece left for his wife. It is common knowledge that Madame Cordet's father paid off his outstanding debts in order that his daughter would not be disgraced.'

'I never heard a word of any of this.'

'I thought Monsieur Verlaine might have told you.'

'Surely you know Grandpère better than that! He never

gossips! Martha says it is because he is a lawyer he has learned the value of a discreet tongue.'

'Well, even if her husband left her nothing, I would still say Madame Cordet was born with a silver spoon in her mouth,' sighed Thérèse. 'She even has the fabulous Monsieur MacIntosh at her beck and call. Tell me, Lucille, are all Scotsmen as handsome as MacIntosh and Sean Connery?'

'No! Not all of them!' I laughed.

'But you know, Lucille,' Thérèse grew serious, 'I should watch out for her with Raoul, if I were you. She is playing him off against MacIntosh, and well, he might get hurt. He is not as sophisticated as Madame Cordet and,' she gave me an anxious look, 'he is a friend, isn't he?'

'If Raoul gets his fingers burned playing with fire, it will teach him a lesson,' I said lightly.

'But – but I thought you and Raoul were – were . . .' her voice trailed off as she met my amused gaze.

'You thought I was interested in Raoul myself?' I laughed. 'You can set your mind at rest, then! Raoul is an amusing acquaintance, nothing more.'

Thérèse heaved a sigh of relief. 'Thank goodness for that! You see, I had imagined you were rather special friends. At least, that was the picture Raoul gave us last year. And I was quite upset just now, when Jacques kept running him down to you. I wondered why you weren't annoyed.'

'I'm not interested in Raoul, or any other man at the moment, Thérèse. I am a career woman, you know. I do not want to get tied up in matrimonial bonds for years and years!'

'That's what you say now,' said Thérèse wisely. 'But wait until you fall in love! Then it will be a different story.'

'Bah!' I laughed. 'I don't believe in falling in love.'

'We'll see!' smiled Thérèse. 'The wonder to me is that you are not affianced already. You are so pretty and gay and—'

'Speak for yourself!' I retorted, and Thérèse giggled and flashed a quick look through the office window to where André was working on a car.

'Ah! So it is André who is the lucky man!' I said, and was going to ask her if the affair was serious, but at that moment, Jacques returned with the Rapier, so I went out to see if he was satisfied that all was in order.

'She is going like a dream,' he assured me. 'And here, have a look at the paintwork.'

He indicated where the car had been scored when it scraped along the rock face on the Col.

'As good as new almost, hein?' he said proudly. 'One would need a suspicious nature and a microscope to detect any damage here.'

'Thanks a lot, Jacques. You have done a wonderful job,' I praised him.

'My pleasure, Lucille,' he smiled. 'I like to please my customers, and more especially my old friends. And talking of old friends,' he went on, 'I have just been having a word with Sergeant Duval.'

'I thought Duval was away in Castellane on business.'

'So he was,' agreed Jacques, 'and was he wild about that! You see, when he went to see his Inspector in Castellane, nothing at all was known about his business! It seems that Duval's phone call to come to town was a hoax!'

'Never!'

'Yes! The police are blaming it on some of the wilder spirits who were at Monsieur Vincennes' party last night, and to whom the good Sergeant gave a severe reprimand for violating local traffic regulations.'

'Oh, how mean!' I cried. 'What a dirty trick!'

'I wouldn't like to be in whoever's shoes it was, if the Sergeant gets hold of him,' said Jacques. 'It takes a lot to rouse old Duval, but Dieu, when he is roused!' He raised his eyes to heaven, 'He has the temper of a fiend!'

I got into the car, thanked Jacques once more, shouted 'A bientôt' to Thérèse, who was chatting to André at the other end of the garage, and drove home.

As I passed the police station, I wondered for a moment if I should stop and go in and have a talk with Duval, as my grandfather had suggested the previous evening, but decided against this in view of the state of the Sergeant's temper as described by Jacques, so I made directly to the Villa Beau Site and drove my car into the back yard, much to the displeasure of the hens which were clucking and scratching there.

Martha looked out of the kitchen window when she heard the car draw up.

'Eh bien,' she said when I came in. 'What happened to you that you should have come home so early, and in your own car? We weren't even expecting you for supper!'

'Madame Cordet wanted to come home early, so I got out at the Villa des Lilas and walked to the garage for my own car.'

'So Madame Cordet was with you, was she?' said Martha with interest. 'How did that work out?'

'Monsieur MacIntosh was there too – not that that made much difference,' I said wryly 'I was still the odd person out.'

'How do you mean?'

'You were right about Raoul, after all. It is Annemarie he is really interested in. He was merely using me to make her jealous.'

'Away with you! He was pleasant enough and eager enough for your company this morning,' she protested. 'Lucille, don't tell me you provoked him into quarrelling with you again! Really!' She went on in exasperation, 'you have no idea how to deal with men! You treat them as equals, which they are not! Men like to be – to be buttered up and flattered and made to feel important! You should take a lesson or two from Madame Cordet.'

'Zut! If a man needs to be buttered and flattered and given boosts to his self-esteem, then he is not the kind of man I want!'

'Then you will live to be an old maid like me!' said Martha glumly. 'I wouldn't be told either.'

'I should rather be an old maid like you, chère Martha,' I gave her a hug, 'than an obnoxious little puss like Madame Cordet!'

Martha looked pleased, but continued none the less to chide me.

'You were never cut out to be an old maid, Lucille. It was different for me. My fiancé was killed in the War and I could find no one to measure up to him. But you have Raoul. You must not let him be taken from you because you are too proud to fight for him.'

'Martha, once and for all, Raoul is nothing to me! Madame Cordet can have him, and welcome!'

I untied my ponytail and let my hair fall loose over my shoulders.

'They are birds of a feather, those two!'

'You sound jealous!' teased Martha. 'And I think that is what Raoul was wanting. He couldn't be genuinely interested in Madame Cordet,' she went on knowingly. 'She is too old for him to be serious about.'

'Martha, you have got it all wrong. Raoul is no more interested in me than I am in him – and even if he was,' I tossed my hair, 'it would make no difference. This afternoon, I saw young Médoc, not through the eyes of an old acquaintance as I have considered him before, but through the eyes of a stranger, and honestly, Martha, I didn't particularly like what I saw.'

I moved restlessly round the room. 'He has grown vain and selfish and ambitious.'

'He will get over it,' said Martha positively. 'Paris always turns a young man's head to begin with. It is like a fever.'

'No, Martha,' I shook my head. 'When I look back, I see he was always a bit like that. He has not the kindness of his father, or the loyalty of young Jacques – or even the courtesy of Greg MacIntosh—'

'Ah!' Martha at me slyly. 'Perhaps you are becoming interested in this other young man, hein?' She nodded her head slowly. 'That might not be a bad thing. He is très agréable, this countryman of yours. Even Monsieur Verlaine has a good word for him.'

'Vraiment!' I cried in despair. 'Why does everyone want to marry me off! You; Grandfather; Thérèse! And what is more, if I had to have a husband, it would be neither Raoul nor this exasperating Monsieur MacIntosh, who treats me as if I were a nit-witted schoolgirl half the time!'

Martha chuckled.

'Perhaps he is right at that!' she agreed. 'Still, I think he would be the very man to keep you in order.'

'Bah!' I exploded. 'You can keep your Raouls and your MacIntoshes! Give me a career instead of a husband any day!'

With that I flounced from the kitchen.

CHAPTER FOURTEEN

I went up to my bedroom to change from my jeans into something which my grandfather would consider more 'convenable' to wear about the house.

I looked morosely through my scanty wardrobe, unable to decide what to put on, and in the end, possibly because my head was still full of thoughts of Greg MacIntosh, and I was annoyed because he treated me more like a teenage schoolgirl than a responsible adult, I chose a black jersey silk dress, very plain and flattering to my fair skin, which I had bought specially for a dinner party given by one of my favourite professors at the University for his star pupils of the year.

The dress made me look, or at least I imagined it made me look, very elegant and woman of the world! Certainly the colour enhanced the youthful bloom of my flesh, and the clever darting emphasized the smallness of my waist, and although it was perhaps rather formal for a mere evening at home with my grandfather, I felt that getting all dressed up, even if I had nowhere to go, would boost my sinking morale.

I brushed my hair back from my face, wound it into a neat bun, and stood back to examine the effect.

I looked as different from the girl with sweety pink jeans and childish ponytail as it was possible to be. Yes. Perhaps I would never look quite so glamorous as Annemarie Cordet with her jet black hair and lustrous dark eyes, but on the whole, I looked not too bad.

Carefully I mascaraed my long lashes, painted my lips a deep rose pink and was dusting a covering of powder over my nose to hide the freckles and across my forehead to disguise the broken skin from my yesterday's fall, when I heard a car draw up outside our front gate.

Since my bedroom faces over the gorge and not the road, I could not peek out to see who was coming to visit, and I couldn't for the life of me imagine anyone in the village paying a call round supper time.

Of course, it might merely be someone who had given my grandfather a lift from the office, and my spirits, which had risen because the visitor might just have been someone to ask me out for the evening, fell again.

I waited to hear if the doorbell would ring or if the car, having deposited Grandfather at his home, would draw away again, and as I stood listening, the sound of voices rose up from the hall below and my grandfather said, 'Come in here for a moment—' and then the lounge door closed and I could hear no more.

Urged by curiosity, I hurried downstairs, opened the front door to see if I knew whose car it was at the gate, and I had the most awful feeling of deflation when I recognized it.

It was Doctor Médoc, Raoul's father, who had come home with Grandpère and not, as I had been stupidly, wishfully hoping, the exasperating Greg MacIntosh.

Hoping!

I repeated the word to myself. Why should I have been hoping that MacIntosh had been the man to give my grandfather a lift home? Why, indeed, should I keep thinking about him all evening? We had only met a few days earlier, and if during that period, we had spent a great deal of time together, it was by chance and not desire.

Martha came up behind me, interrupting my puzzled thoughts.

'Did I hear Monsieur Verlaine arrive home?' she asked.

'Yes, Martha. I heard his voice, and since Doctor Médoc's car is at the door, I think he must be in the lounge with Grandpapa.'

I started to follow Martha back across the hall but she barred my way and stood looking at me critically.

'Tiens!' she said. 'You did not tell me you were going out again.'

'But I'm not!' I responded lightly. 'I hope to spend a quiet evening here with Grandpère.'

'Pah!' proclaimed Martha. 'No one dresses up like that for a grandfather!' She gave my a sly look. 'You are not, by any chance, hoping that your Raoul will call to kiss and make up?'

'Don't be silly!' I protested, flushing.

'We shall see!' Martha nodded knowingly. 'We shall see! Oh, and by the way, Lucille, perhaps you would find out if your grandfather has invited Doctor Médoc to join us for supper. I hope he has! That poor man could do with a well cooked meal for a change.'

'What you mean, Martha,' I smiled teasingly, 'is that you want someone else to praise your culinary expertise!' and before she could reply, I whisked into the lounge.

I kissed Grandfather's cheeks and went forward, hand outstretched, to greet Doctor Médoc.

'Bon soir, Monsieur Médoc,' I said with a smile, but the doctor made no move to take my proffered hand.

He looked as white and shocked as if he was looking at a ghost, and I was so taken aback at his expression, that I hesitated, and said apologetically,

'Oh dear! I hope I didn't startle you, dashing into the room as I did.'

Grandfather interrupted me.

'Eugène!' he cried. 'What is the matter? You look ill!'

'It's – it's nothing,' said the doctor, but his ashen face belied his words. 'I – I have had one or two such odd turns recently. That is why I have made up my mind to retire.'

'Oh! So Raoul was right. He was saying something about it, but we found it difficult to believe.'

'I came tonight to tell you about my plans,' Médoc's voice was stronger, but his hands were still trembling and his face remained a ghastly grey.

'Lucille,' Grandfather touched my arm, 'fetch the brandy. Eugène,' he turned to his old friend, 'I did not realize how ill you were. Come! Sit down over here,' he guided him to a chair. 'You should be taking things easy when you are in this condition.'

He looked down at his friend with anxious eyes.

'Actually,' he went on, 'these past few days when I have seen you in the street, I have thought that all was not well with you.'

'I shall be all right in a moment,' Médoc took the glass of brandy from my hand. 'Sometimes I get over-tired.'

Personally, I thought there was a great deal more than over-tiredness to the doctor's condition, but I said nothing, not wishing to upset him further.

'You are back a lot earlier than I had expected, Lucille,' Grandfather adroitly changed the subject. 'Was the beach too crowded for you? The summer season at Cannes begins earlier each year.'

'It wasn't at all busy where we were, but Annemarie wanted to come home early, so' – I shrugged – 'that was that!'

'Ah! So Madame Cordet was with you as well as Raoul. I didn't know that.'

'Mr MacIntosh made up the foursome,' I told him.

'Mr MacIntosh? Now, there's an extremely likeable young fellow,' said Grandfather.

'Madame Cordet certainly agrees with you there!'

'So that's the way of it, is it?' said Grandfather. 'I wondered when I saw them constantly together last night. Yes!' he nodded. 'That would be a good match. MacIntosh is the kind of man who would be able to manage a woman like that, and also, it would be a convenient arrangement for Monsieur Vincennes too, to have a son-in-law with an interest in his firm.'

'What do you mean?' I asked in surprise.

'Didn't I tell you? It is one of Monsieur Vincennes' companies which has the contract for our new highway, and MacIntosh is one of the principal engineers attached to it.'

'I didn't know about that!' I walked over to the window and looked out thoughtfully. 'I couldn't understand why they were all so friendly.'

Médoc's harsh voice broke into my train of thought.

'Did MacIntosh drive Madame Cordet home?' he demanded.

'Beg pardon?' I said, bringing my mind back to the conversation.

'Was Madame Cordet with MacIntosh?' the doctor repeated, quite sharply

'No. As a matter of fact, we decided to change partners on the way back, because Annemarie prefers Raoul's driving, so I came with Greg, but I left them all at the Villa des Lilas, because I wanted to go to Jacques' garage to collect my own car,' I explained.

'Ah!' Médoc let out a long exhalation, almost as if he was relieved about something, and I shot him a puzzled look.

Why was he so interested in who had been with whom? Was he aware of his own son's interest in the pretty girl from Paris, and was he hoping that something might come of it?

'Our good doctor has been telling me, Lucille,' my grandfather entered the conversation, 'that he went up to see our friend Jules this afternoon.'

'You did?' I exclaimed. 'Did he let you in?'

'Si. Today he did not slam the door in my face. Instead he was pleased to see me and accept the medicine I brought for him.'

The colour was returning to the doctor's face and he spoke with more animation.

'Poor Jules has had some sort of fever which has been making him have hallucinations, and act strangely.'

Grandfather agreed. 'Yes. He was behaving most peculiarly when I saw him at the beginning of last week. As a matter of fact, he looked as if he was afraid of something.'

'People who live alone are inclined to panic when they fall

ill,' answered Médoc. 'However, Jules is better now, though still quite weak.'

'He looked very odd when I saw him through the window of the shack yesterday afternoon,' I said. 'I hardly recognized him! And his manner!' I frowned.

'What is puzzling you, Lucille?' asked Grandfather.

'I don't know,' I hesitated. 'There was something about Jules that worried me. It seemed not right, if you know what I mean, but I can't think what it was! However, I daresay it will come to mind sometime, and meantime, it is nice to know he is better again. I must call and see him tomorrow, and take him some of Martha's soup to build up his strength.'

'No!' the word almost exploded from the doctor's lips. 'You must not go near Jules, Lucille! Nor you either, for that matter, mon ami,' he turned to my grandfather. 'This fever from which Lamartine is suffering is most infectious. I want no one near his shack until he is completely well again, in case we start an epidemic in the village.'

'Nonsense!' I said. 'I work with the Red Cross in Edinburgh. I am used to illness. I am sure I could be of some help to Jules. Why!' I shook my head. 'You simply cannot leave that poor soul alone in his isolated shack, night and day, with no one to attend to him.'

'No!' Médoc was firm. 'It is my duty, as doctor for the neighbourhood, to keep this illness from spreading. I will not let you run unnecessary risks, Lucille. I myself shall call twice daily on Lamartine until he is well again.'

'Mon ami!' objected my grandfather. 'You are scarcely fit enough to look after yourself at the moment, never mind playing nursemaid to Jules! If you won't let either Lucille or myself lend him a hand, how about Mère Picard? I know she is not fit for very much, but I have no doubt that, for a small fee, she would be willing and able to keep Lamartine's shack tidy, make him some hot gruel, and milk and feed his goats.'

'You know how Lamartine hates strangers nosing around,' said Médoc.

'Mère Picard is hardly a stranger!' laughed Grandfather.

'Surely you have not forgotten how closely she and Lamartine worked together in the Resistance?'

'Leave it meantime,' said Médoc. 'I'll see what Jules is like tomorrow. If he is worse, I'll have a word with Mère Picard myself. If he is better—'

'If he is better,' I put in quickly, 'I shall be able to do something for him. After all, I owe Jules Lamartine more than I can ever repay.' I laughed self-consciously. 'If it hadn't been for him, after all, my father would never have got on to the escape route to Switzerland, and then I would not be here today!'

'Yes,' Doctor Médoc looked at me. 'You are lucky to be alive today, Lucille. Very lucky,' he repeated, and drained his glass of brandy.

'I must be on my way now,' he put down the glass and stood up. 'Thank you for your kindness.'

He shook hands with Grandfather and gave me a courteous bow.

'Do not worry about Jules,' he said. 'I will look after him, and let you know how he is getting on.'

He took his leave.

CHAPTER FIFTEEN

'That man is a bundle of nerves,' remarked Grandfather, when he returned to the lounge after seeing his visitor to the front door. 'The fact is, Madame Médoc is so wrapped up in herself, and her beloved son, she does not bother to look after him properly.'

'You know, Grandfather,' I said, moving out on to the terrace where the bats were already beginning their nocturnal forays, 'it's odd how Raoul is so different from his father, both in looks and personality.'

Grandpère followed me into the garden and we stood leaning against the balustrade, looking out across the black chasm of the gorge to the dark grey outlines of the hills beyond.

'No,' he agreed. 'There doesn't appear to be a single Médoc characteristic in him. His looks and personality are all from his mother's side.'

'A pity,' I sighed.

Grandfather looked at me, but said nothing, and for several minutes, each engaged with our own thoughts, we stood staring into the gloom, with the noise of the waters of the Lune as they tossed and tumbled unseen over the rocks far below us, the only noise to distract our thinking.

'Lucille,' Grandpapa said softly at last, 'is it finally all over between you and Raoul?'

'There was never any deep feeling on my side,' I reassured him. 'Raoul was only a habit. Someone of my own age to amuse me on holiday. The boy next door.' I gestured with my hand to the stark outline of a house which stood a couple of hundred yards beyond ours.

'When we were young, it was fun to play together and climb over the rocks from one house to the next. Now I am grown up, and a man and woman have to have a firmer basis for friendship, never mind marriage, than an age group and a neighbouring garden.'

'So!'

'You are disappointed?'

'I didn't want to influence you, chérie, but somehow I never thought you would settle with Raoul. You have too much commonsense for a gambler like that!'

'Grandpapa! You make me sound dull!'

He chuckled. 'Lucille, with a temper like yours, you could never be dull! There are even times when I feel quite sorry for the man who will one day marry you!'

From inside the house came the rumble of the dinner gong.

Grandpapa took my arm.

'Poor Martha will be disappointed! She always hoped that you and Raoul would make a match of it.'

'Don't you believe it!' I laughed. 'Since I have told her it is over between us, she is already looking out for someone else for me!'

We did justice to Martha's excellent meal and had just finished and gone into the lounge to await our after dinner coffee, when there was a ring at the front door.

'I wonder who that can be at this time?' Grandfather looked at me in surprise. 'I was expecting no one. Were you?'

I shook my head.

Martha came into the room, looking flustered.

'It's Sergeant Duval,' she said, 'and Monsieur MacIntosh,' she shot me a queer look. 'They wish a word with you.'

'Show them in here, please, Martha,' said Grandfather, 'and bring two extra cups with the coffee.'

She nodded and, seconds later, Duval came into the lounge, followed by Greg, who was still wearing the gay tartan shirt he had worn to Cannes.

Duval shook hands with my grandfather and myself, but Greg only shook hands with Grandfather.

I indicated two vacant chairs and Greg chose the one nearer to me, although he pushed it back as he sat down so that while he could see me, I would have had to turn round to look at him.

'Well, gentlemen?' Grandfather looked from one to the other. 'What can I do for you?'

Sergeant Duval pursed his lips.

'I do not know where to begin, Monsieur Verlaine,' he said gravely. 'So many things have been happening. So many strange things,' he shot me a worried look.

'It is always best, is it not, to start at the beginning?' suggested Grandfather.

'The beginning?' Duval shrugged. 'Who knows where the whole thing starts?'

I looked at Grandpapa, who seemed as puzzled as I.

'However,' went on Duval slowly, 'I shall start with today. This morning I received a telephone call which asked me, as a matter of urgency, to call on my superior in Castellane.'

'We heard of that. It is why I didn't come to see you,' I interrupted.

'Ah, yes!' Duval nodded. 'I think that was part of the pattern.'

I was more mystified than ever.

'What do you mean?'

'This! When I arrived in Castellane, mademoiselle, no one knew anything of any telephone call. My superior was not on duty! No one wished to see me! I had had my journey for nothing.'

'So!' Grandfather eyed him keenly.

'Naturally, at first I thought the affair was some stupid person's idea of a joke.

'Last night, you see, I had occasion to reprimand several of Monsieur Vincennes' younger guests about their driving. One or two were annoyed. Others were rude and called me a stupid, country bumpkin.'

I felt my lips twitch, but managed to control the smile.

'I could have been awkward, vous savez, but it was not worth it. All I wanted was for those people to get safely away from Tourloup before there were any accidents. One young man, however, insisted on ignoring the yellow line repeatedly, so I fined him on the spot.

'He was rather drunk and vowed he would get his own back.'

'So you thought he was the joker?'

'Exactly!' Duval nodded. 'I was extremely angry. I had wasted my entire morning in a wild goose chase, and the moment I got back to my station, I looked up this young man's name and address in my book and tried to contact him by telephone. He was not at home, but his mother, who answered the call, assured me that her son had flown from Nice only that morning to London, and could not possibly have telephoned to me at the relevant time.'

'Who else could it have been?'

'I'm coming to that. You see, during the afternoon I happened to meet Monsieur Vincennes. He did not know I had been at Castellane and he went on to say,' and here the Sergeant paused dramatically, ' "I see you were sufficiently interested in the new story Miss Mathieson told you to institute another search for the body in the river"!'

I gaped at him. 'But—' I began, but the sergeant held up a hand for silence.

'I asked Monsieur Vincennes what made him think I had renewed the search.

'He told me he had taken his daughter's dog for a walk earlier in the day, through the high woods. From the top of a ridge he had a clear view of that part of the Lune above the rapids, and he saw three people down by the river, systematically searching along the banks with sticks. One of the persons was on the far side of the river.'

'Yes?' Duval had our full attention.

'Monsieur Vincennes saw the man on the far side signal his companions and point downstream. The other two ran forward and went wading knee deep into the river, to a point where some dead branches and weeds had become tangled, and were blocking the near side of the river.

'As he watched, these people pulled something away from a pool dammed up by waste material, and together they carried back to the shore what he swears could only be a body!'

I gasped, but Grandfather said, frowning,

'Surely, if someone had found the body, it would have been reported to you right away.'

Duval looked at us gravely.

'It should have been,' he agreed. 'And doubtless it would have been, if anyone else had found it. But you see these people who were searching so carefully by the river did not want me, or anyone else, to see that particular body, in case it was indentified!'

I stared at him, mouth agape.

'Don't you see,' he went on, 'that was why I was called away to Castellane! It was to give these men a chance to find the body before Mademoiselle Mathieson came to me and insisted on a new search!'

'It doesn't make sense!' I looked from Duval to Grandfather. 'After all, no one tried to stop your first search.'

Duval flushed.

'To be honest, Mademoiselle Mathieson, when you came to me with your story of what you had found in the river, I thought you were telling a bit of a tall story. I mean to say, we knew no one was missing from Tourloup, or its neighbourhood, and as young Médoc said at the time, you have always been noted for your imagination.

'So,' he avoided my eyes, 'I went by myself to have a look. I had a fairly good idea where the "body", if it was a body, might show up, and I was walking along the river bank towards this spot, when I found the scarecrow.'

'And you put two and two together!'

'As he was meant to!' Greg spoke for the first time. 'Someone did a bit of quick thinking there. They knew your story would sound far-fetched, Lucille, and they relied on a perfunctory search which would quickly find the substitute scarecrow.'

'It was a clever ruse to throw me off the track, and it succeeded,' said Duval.

'Only for the time being, however, because you, Lucille,' said Greg gravely, 'refused to be turned into a figure of fun. You were determined to prove you were right. At the party last night, you said very clearly that if Duval wouldn't look again, you would yourself, so they simply had to find their elusive victim!'

'But who are these people?' I demanded. 'And who was their victim? And – oh dear – it all sounds far too melodramatic to be real!'

'It may be melodrama to you, my dear, but it is actually fact,' said Greg positively.

'Yes, mademoiselle,' said Duval, 'no one is imagining all this! You see, we now have proof that something very odd is happening in this area, and you have innocently been caught up in a web of intrigue which has already almost cost you your life.'

'What!' I squeaked.

Greg pulled his chair forward so that he was sitting directly alongside of me, and he took hold of my hand in the comforting, in fact almost protective, way he had done after our near escape on the Col road that afternoon.

'Lucille,' he said gravely, 'I have something to add to the Sergeant's story. Something which confirms the fact that you have stumbled on a curious and dangerous situation; something which confirms that the shot which so narrowly missed you yesterday afternoon was fired, not by accident, but in earnest.'

'Bon Dieu!' exploded Grandfather. 'What do you mean by that?'

Greg's pressure on my hand increased.

'Lucille will tell you that this afternoon she and I narrowly escaped being killed on the road near the pass by a boulder which tumbled down from the cliff face.'

Grandfather's face went white.

'Lucille! Child! Why didn't you tell me?'

'I didn't have a chance and, in any case, I wanted to forget about it.'

Greg gave me an admiring smile, which made me feel good inside.

'What a girl!' Then he grew serious again.

'Lucille, remember at the time I told you I could not understand how there could be a landslide at that particular part, because of the tilt of the land?'

I nodded. 'Yes, but—'

'No buts, my child! I know you thought out some plausible explanation, but it didn't satisfy me. After I left you this afternoon—'

'You went for a drink with Annemarie!' I said, pulling my hand from his grasp.

'After that,' Greg continued unperturbed, 'my curiosity was so aroused, I went back to the Col and climbed to the top to see from where the boulder had come adrift.'

He paused and looked from Duval to Grandfather, and finally to me.

'Lucille, that stone had not rolled over the cliff of its own accord. It had been prised from its actual resting place – the marks of the lever still showed up clearly, though I could detect no definite footprints – and levered along the two or three yards that separated it from the edge, where it must have been deliberately shoved over when our car appeared below!'

CHAPTER SIXTEEN

'I don't believe it!' I said flatly. 'You are making it up!'

'No,' said Sergeant Duval crisply. 'Monsieur MacIntosh is telling the truth. Directly he had examined the spot where the rock came from, he came seeking me and brought me back to have a look at the evidence for myself.

'I came to the same conclusion he had come to, and also, I realized that the telephone call which had taken me to Castellane had not been a foolish hoax, but a deliberate attempt to get me out of the way for the crucial hours required to recover the body, so that is why, Mademoiselle Mathieson, I have come to you tonight.'

He paused. 'You have stumbled on something no one was meant even to suspect. Some plot which the plotters are so determined to keep under cover that twice determined attempts have been made on your life. Why you should be such a deadly embarrassment to them I do not know—'

'It is because Lucille had an idea she had seen their victim somewhere before! They were afraid she would remember where,' exclaimed Grandfather.

'You what!' cried Duval. 'You never told me this story!'

'That was what I was coming to tell you this morning, when you were so conveniently spirited away!'

'But if you recognized the dead man, why did you not tell me so in the first place?' said Duval angrily. 'Then I wouldn't have been put off by the scarecrow.'

I looked at him helplessly.

'Because – it's difficult to explain – you see, I didn't actually recognize the face. As I told you first of all, it was no one I could identify and I thought when you did recover it, some relative would, so there seemed no point in stressing the fact that I thought there was something familiar about the face. It reminded me of someone!'

Duval stroked his chin.

'I wonder. Is it possible you had seen not the man, but a photograph of him at some time, and that was why he looked familiar?'

'That could be,' I said cautiously.

'What have you in mind, Duval?' questioned Grandfather.

'You remember the Ben Kader affair?' said Duval. 'The kidnapping of the Algerian politician on his visit to Marseilles at the beginning of the year.'

'Yes,' Grandfather frowned. 'You don't think there is any connection surely?'

'Neither Kader, nor his right-hand man, have ever turned up. Not even their bodies!' Duval spoke slowly. 'What is more, it has often been rumoured that the kidnappers had their headquarters somewhere north of Nice.'

'Bon Dieu!' Grandfather expelled a long breath. 'If that were the case, no wonder the kidnappers did not want a body to turn up which could be recognized!'

'And they certainly did not want someone who had actually seen the body to be a continual thorn in their flesh!' said Duval. 'That is why they have tried, thank goodness unsuccessfully, to get rid of your grand-daughter.'

I fumbled for Greg MacIntosh's comforting hand and clasped it tightly, and then aware of my grandfather's surprised look at this demonstration, I hurriedly let go of it again, and pushed my chair away from his.

'Surely, now they know you are on to them, they will give up trying?' I said anxiously.

Duval hesitated. 'That is what worries me,' he looked across at Grandfather, as if for guidance. 'Even if, this very night, we showed you pictures of Ben Kader, and you identified him as the man whose body you found, you could still be a danger until we catch those unknowns, and bring them to trial.' He cleared his throat. 'If you were to die before then, you see, we should have no witness to testify against them.'

I felt myself go cold.

'Do you think it would be better then, if Lucille returned to Scotland? Until these men are caught, I mean?' asked Grandfather.

Duval shook his head. 'We don't even know whom we are looking for,' he said dejectedly. 'For all we know, your grand-daughter's life could be in danger, no matter where she goes.'

'They certainly must have been following her pretty closely this afternoon,' said Greg. 'It was only at the last minute she came home with me instead of her boy-friend, yet they knew which car to ambush!'

I shivered.

'What am I to do?' I looked from one anxious face to the other. 'Lock myself in my bedroom for the rest of my life?'

'No!' Duval returned my glance. 'I came to you here for a specific reason. I wish to ask a favour of you.'

'What is that?' barked Grandfather.

'These people, whoever they are, do not realize I know about them. Monsieur MacIntosh here will say nothing of his investigation of the landslide.'

'I don't follow?' I said puzzled.

'Mademoiselle, as long as these people think we are unaware of their activities, they will not seek to draw attention to themselves by committing murder openly.

'These two attempts on your life so far could have been taken for accidents, n'est-ce pas?'

We all nodded.

'It is not easy to arrange a "successful" fatal accident as they have already found out, but they must try again. Only, this time, we shall be ready for them!'

'You want Miss Mathieson to be a guinea pig, is that it?' said Greg MacIntosh angrily. 'I don't like the idea at all.'

'Ni moi non plus!' roared Grandfather. 'I say, either give her full police protection, or let her go back to Scotland out of danger.'

'Police protection would draw attention to the fact we are on to them,' said Duval stolidly. 'Then they might have no compunction in murdering her in cold blood, at any time of the day or night.'

Grandfather paced up and down the room, muttering to himself.

'If I could get my hands on the villains!' he ranted.

Greg lit another cigarette.

'It's the devil!' he said explosively. 'Whatever way we play it, Lucille is in danger.'

There was another silence.

'Sergeant Duval,' I said shakily. 'Do you think your plan would work?'

Grandpère stopped his pacing, and Greg drew in a hissing breath.

'Accidents can be avoided if we look out for them,' Duval looked steadily at me. 'And all the time, someone would be constantly on the lookout to see who springs the trap.'

'No!' objected Grandfather. 'You can't use Lucille as live bait!'

'It would depend,' said Greg cautiously. 'Someone would have to be with her, day and night, until we catch them.'

'It would have to look natural, though,' said Duval. 'By night, she should be safe enough. For example, she could move the position of her bed, or even sleep in a different room.'

'And by day, she could go with her grandfather to the office, or I could go along with her, if she was going elsewhere.'

'Raoul could help out too, I'm sure,' said Grandpapa.

'No,' disagreed Duval. 'Young Médoc is a newspaper man. There might be too big a story in this for him to keep it to himself.'

'How long will it go on for?' I asked dolefully.

'Not long!' promised Duval. 'All we have to look out for

are strangers who display too great a degree of interest in you. Then we should be able to do something.'

'That shouldn't be difficult, surely!' I felt a wave of relief. 'Strangers in Tourloup at this time would stand out like a sore thumb.'

'We didn't see any strangers in the wood when that shot was fired at you,' said Greg doubtfully.

'We weren't looking very hard, were we?'

'I still don't like it,' said Grandfather. 'If anything should happen to Lucille, I'd never forgive myself, or you, Sergeant Duval, and especially you! If you had bothered to look properly for the body in the first place, we wouldn't be facing our present dilemma!'

There was a tap at the door and Martha came in with the coffee.

'Eh bien,' she looked at Duval. 'Has Lucille managed to convince you it wasn't a scarecrow she saw?'

Duval hesitated, then, tipping us the wink not to say anything even to Martha, he said briskly, 'I'm afraid not, Martha. I still think she was letting her imagination run riot, and I have had enough hoaxes played on me for one day, not to fall for another!'

Martha looked quite taken aback by his scepticism, and I added with a shrug,

'The Sergeant is a hard man to convince, Martha, so I am saying no more.'

'It had nothing to do with you anyway,' she sounded relieved. 'I'd forget all about it if I were you,' and with that she set down the coffee tray and retired from the room.

While I poured, at Duval's suggestion Grandfather went to his study and returned with a pile of back numbers of *Paris Match* for me to look through, to see if I could recognize Ben Kader's photo in any of the news pieces written at the time of his disappearance.

However, I couldn't honestly say I saw any resemblance between the photographs of any of the men involved, and the face of the man in the river, and at length Duval gave up and went away.

Greg MacIntosh made no move to go. He and Grandpère seemed to be enjoying each other's company, and while I continued to search fruitlessly through the back numbers of *Paris Match*, they discussed the new road project and other jobs on which Greg had worked in different parts of the world.

After a time I laid down my magazines, and sat quietly listening as he talked of the faraway places to which his work had taken him – Arabia and Iran, Siam and the Sahara – and as these places took shape for me as he described them with the eye of the interested observer, I forgot about the present, and the threat under which I was living, lulled to a sense of security by the fascinating lilt of Greg's Highland-French accent.

All too soon, he decided it was time to leave.

'We have enjoyed your company this evening, Monsieur MacIntosh,' my grandfather stood up. 'We should be glad if you would visit us again soon.'

'Thank you, sir, I should be pleased to,' replied Greg.

Grandfather moved towards the door, and Greg came over to me and shook hands formally, in the French manner.

'Bon soir, Lucille,' he smiled at me. 'In many ways, this has been a most pleasant evening. But, you know,' his eyes twinkled teasingly, 'I hardly recognized you when I came into the room, you look so grown up!'

His glance approved my dress and hair style.

'I am grown up!' I retorted. 'And I do wish you would stop looking on me as if I were a backward adolescent!'

'Oh!' Greg's brows shot up. 'Is that how you think I see you?' He regarded me with a quizzical smile. 'I wonder what gives you that impression?'

'As if you didn't know!' I flashed back. 'Why—' and here I stopped, taken aback by the odd expression in his eyes, and, as his gaze held mine, he took a step forward and for one incredible moment I felt sure that in spite of Grandfather's presence he was going to kiss me, but he stopped, his face close to mine, and said soberly,

'Please be careful, Lucille. I should hate anything to

happen to you,' and with that he turned abruptly and followed my grandfather from the room, leaving me to stare after him in surprise.

I could not for the life of me understand the moods of this unfairly attractive man, whose very presence made me tingle with a peculiar awareness of him, and yet who provoked me so that we could scarcely be together for any length of time without arguing.

I walked over to the window, against which a myriad of moths and other insects of the night were beating in vain, and gazed blankly out into the darkness, trying to dismiss every thought of Greg MacIntosh from my mind, while I waited for my grandfather to return from seeing his visitor off, but I had a long time to wait for the two men stood in the vestibule for a considerable period, talking in low voices.

When Grandfather did eventually come back to the lounge, he was looking tired and thoughtful. He came over to stand beside me, and he, too, looked blankly out into the night as if he was thinking over his recent conversation.

At last, he spoke quietly.

'It is good to have someone like Monsieur MacIntosh on one's side,' he put an affectionate arm round my shoulder.

'You know, Lucille, he reminds me very much of your father. He is a man of courage and kindliness. Yes,' he nodded, and then, briskly, 'but it is late, my dear. High time you were in bed if you are to accompany me to the office in the morning!'

With that, he kissed me on both cheeks, and bade me 'Good night'.

CHAPTER SEVENTEEN

It didn't take me many minutes to undress, wash off my make-up and get in between the cool, lavender-scented sheets, but I did not fall asleep right away.

I could hear Grandfather going round the house, carefully testing each lock at door and window, and I shrank into myself when I realized the reason for this unusual carefulness.

Normally, in Tourloup, you can leave doors and windows unlocked night and day, even if the house is empty, and the sound of each bolt being shot, and each key being turned, underlined for me the danger which threatened me, so that I got out of my bed and pushed it into the far corner of the room, where it was out of sight of the window, for even though the window was shuttered, I reckoned that the slats were wide enough for a resolute person to aim through and, even if Sergeant Duval appeared sure my death would be made to look like an accident, I was determined to run no risks.

I crept back into bed again. Now the house was still, save for the familiar creaks and groans that furniture makes from time to time, and only the moonlight intruded through the slats of the shutters, making a geometric pattern of light and shade on the floor and glinting off a golden hairpin which had fallen to the ground as I had unwound my sophisticated hair-do.

At least, I thought sleepily, Greg had noticed the difference in my appearance, and he had liked what he saw.

Greg. I didn't want to think of him. I determined not to think of him, and yet I could not help myself and in trying to determine what that odd glance of his, as he had stepped forward to say good night, meant, I forgot to think about the frightening reason that had made him call on us and, still thinking of him, I fell asleep.

Grandfather himself came to waken me next morning. I stirred as he gently shook my shoulder.

'Lucille! Lucille!' he called. 'If you are to come with me to the office this morning, you will have to get up now!'

I opened my eyes, rubbed the sleep away and struggled to wakefulness.

'To the office?' I repeated, stifling a yawn. 'What – oh!' memory dawned.

I sat up. 'I'll not be five minutes, Grandpapa,' I stretched. 'Does Martha know why I am going with you?'

'No. The fewer people who are in the know, the better. In any case, why worry more friends than we need to?' he said sensibly. 'So now, up with you! No lying back for another few seconds!' He smiled and left the room.

A cold mist from the high snows had drifted down during the night and eddied thickly in patches over the hillside and in the gorge.

When the mists roll down, it can be chilly in Tourloup, so I put on my warmest dress, a poppy red wool shift, and went down to breakfast.

This morning, naturally, there was no thought of eating out of doors. We sat in the small dining-room and I enjoyed a cup of hot chocolate with my croissants, while grandfather skimmed through the local newspaper.

This reminded me of the news item I had read in the paper which lined the drawer of the dressing-table in my bedroom.

'Grandfather, did you know Major Haabe had been released from prison?'

He looked at me over the top of his newspaper.

'Yes,' he said shortly. 'Who was telling you?'

'I read about it.' I helped myself to another roll. 'What do people here say about him?'

'The war is over a long time, Lucille,' he said firmly. 'There are new generations in Tourloup to whom the name means nothing, and the older generation do not want to remember a painful past.'

'You don't suppose he would ever have the nerve to come back here, do you?'

'To look for the legendary loot he is said to have taken from the Mercredis and buried?' Grandfather laughed. 'After the war, there were plenty of hopeful fortune hunters, who came here to look for the lost treasures of the Mercredis, and other valuables Haabe was reputed to have stolen and buried near here, but no one ever found anything.'

I carefully balanced a pat of butter on the crescent tip of my roll.

'They wouldn't have an idea where to begin to look, but Haabe might think he knew!'

'I doubt very much if Heinrich Haabe would dare show his face in this village again for all the gold, silver and jewellery in France,' he declared. 'I know I said we do not want to remember a painful past, but if that past was forced to our recall by the presence of a monster like Haabe,' Grandfather's face changed before my eyes from the jovial, benevolent man I had known all my life to the cold, tight-lipped, remorseless face of a stranger. 'There are those who would see to it he did not leave here again.'

I shivered, and the movement sent the pat of butter jerkily off the roll I was about to bite into.

For the rest of the meal, Grandfather sat in silence, his eyes on the printed page in front of him, but the expression on his face told me he was not reading the news of the day. His mind was still back in the grim times of quarter of a century earlier.

A ring at the doorbell disturbed us both, and we were equally surprised when Martha announced the arrival of Raoul Médoc.

'Show him in, Martha,' said Grandfather, 'and bring another cup.' He looked at me. 'I thought you said you had given this young man his congé, Lucille?'

'So I did!' I exclaimed. 'I wonder what on earth he wants this time, and at this hour of the morning,' I glanced at the enormous cuckoo clock in the corner, which pointed to a few minutes after eight o'clock.

'You don't think his father has taken a really bad turn?' I added as an anxious afterthought. 'He looked very far from well when he left us last night.'

'That could be it,' Grandfather frowned.

He stood up as Raoul himself entered the room.

'Bonjour, Raoul,' he shook hands with the doctor's son. 'You are an early visitor?' his voice rose in a question.

'I hope I haven't disturbed you,' Raoul came forward to shake my hand, but I blandly ignored the gesture by conscientiously spreading another layer of cherry jam on to the roll in front of me.

After the way he had used me yesterday, Master Médoc would have to apologize very nicely before I would be civil to him again.

He looked annoyed at the rebuff, but recovered himself quickly.

'Bonjour, Lucille,' his charming smile did not reach his angry eyes. 'I did not expect to see you up so soon.'

'I am going to help Grandfather in his office. I thought it might be a good idea to have some practical training, you understand, before I take up a secretarial course at a London college.'

'You have your future neatly arranged, don't you?' he sneered.

'What brings you here so early?' Grandfather impatiently interrupted our cross talk. 'Is it your father? Lucille was just remarking to me that he looked far from well when he took his leave of us last night.'

'Father is all right,' replied Raoul. 'He worries too much, that is his trouble.'

'And Madame Médoc? How is she? Has her migraine disappeared sufficiently to let her get out and about again?' I asked.

'What do you mean?' he demanded sharply.

I looked at him in surprise. 'It *was* an attack of migraine which made your mother leave the party the other evening, wasn't it? And usually such attacks leave her laid up for a few days.'

'Maman is still confined to bed, if that is what you mean,' said Raoul. 'I think it is more from boredom than anything else she stays there. She will be a different woman once we settle down at the coast and she finds more things to interest her.'

'Your father was confirming what you told me earlier about his retirement,' said Grandfather, signing to Martha, who had come in with a fresh pot of coffee, to fill up a cup for Raoul. 'He doesn't expect to stay on here many more months.'

'No. It is all decided now,' said Raoul, sipping his coffee, while I added more chocolate and cream to my own cup before saying, sweetly,

'You still haven't told us why you have honoured us with such an early visit, Raoul? Don't tell me you are thinking of going to Cannes again?'

'On a day like this?' Raoul looked out at the swirling mists. 'You would have to crawl over the Col, and I haven't the patience for that kind of thing! No. Why I came is – I have mislaid my lighter, and I was wondering if I had left it here yesterday morning, by any chance?'

'Martha would have noticed,' said Grandfather.

'Didn't you have it at the Carlton? I am almost certain I saw you use it there,' I said. 'Yes, I'm positive! You lit a cigarette for Annemarie with it.'

'In that case, I had better phone the Carlton and see if I dropped it there. I shouldn't like to lose it.'

'Didn't you have it insured? It was pure gold, wasn't it?'

'I don't like losing anything,' said Raoul, 'and talking of losing things, has old Duval found the body you lost yet?' his tone was joking.

I bit into my roll, giving myself time to think out a suitable answer. I had been warned to let no hint of last night's discussion reach Raoul's inquisitive ears, so once my mouth was free of food, I replied lightly,

'I'm afraid Sergeant Duval still thinks I am romancing! He called here last night to tell me as much.'

'So he does not intend to institute a fresh search?' asked Raoul.

'He said that frankly he has not the time to waste on a further wild goose chase!'

'And you? What did you say to this?'

'The truth is, Raoul, that I am now sick to death of the whole affair, and I mean to forget about it, so please, no more on the subject, hein?'

Grandfather flashed me an approving look, before saying, 'Raoul, if you will excuse us, we must be on our way. I do not wish to keep my first client waiting.'

He pushed back his chair and rose to his feet.

'Is Lucille really going to the office with you?' Raoul said in amazement. 'I thought she was pulling my leg!'

'I was being perfectly serious,' I assured him. 'In any case, what else would there be to do on a day like this?'

'Annemarie has asked me to play table tennis with her in their games room. You could come and join us, if you like,' he suggested generously. 'I'm sure she wouldn't mind.'

'No?' I said doubtfully.

'You are coming with me,' said Grandfather firmly. 'No backing out now!'

'What about this afternoon?' persisted Raoul.

'I am waiting to hear what your father has to say about Jules Lamartine. If he is better, I shall go to see him this afternoon. You can come with me if you like.'

'You can leave off seeing Jules for another day,' said Grandfather. 'It is time you visited Madame de Jarenté. She is completely bed-ridden, and it would be a kindness if you were to spend a few hours with her this afternoon.'

'Of course,' I agreed at once. 'I shall look out some of my latest magazines for her. She always likes to be au courant with the latest trends and fashions!'

'But what about me?' Raoul sounded quite peeved. 'When shall I be able to see you, Lucille?'

'See me?' I raised my eyebrows. 'Has Annemarie lost interest in you?' I spoke maliciously.

'I only said what I did to you yesterday to make you jealous,' he sounded sullen. 'You didn't need to go off with MacIntosh.'

'What!' I gasped. 'It was you who went off with Annemarie!'

'Mes enfants!' intervened Grandfather. 'Will the pair of you stop your quarrelling? At least, for the moment. Lucille, I shall be late for my appointment if we don't leave now, and Raoul,' he went on kindly, 'I am sure Lucille will have time for you tomorrow, hein?' he asked me. 'You could visit Jules together, if the doctor has no objection.'

'Surely we could do something more interesting than pass the time of day with an old recluse!' He turned the full charm of his smile on me. 'I'll think of something, believe me!'

CHAPTER EIGHTEEN

I spent an unexpectedly busy morning in Grandfather's office.

His clerk showed me the filing system, and I checked her letters before handing them to Grandpapa for signature, and I answered the telephone. It was answering calls which took up most of my time.

Sergeant Duval himself telephoned three times to see that I was all right, and that nothing out of the way had taken place.

The third time he got in touch with us was to say that he had contacted Paris about the Ben Kader affair, but there they were of the opinion the men responsible had fled the country. They also told Duval, as a matter of interest, that they had received a routine report from Interpol that Heinrich Haabe, the German war criminal, had disappeared from the Geneva convalescent home where he had gone after his release, and his present whereabouts were unknown. In view of his connection with Tourloup, they thought they would pass the word on to Duval.

Now Duval was wondering if the body I had found could have been that of the Major, and he was wondering when it would be suitable for him to come to the office with some photographs of Haabe he had in his files!

Grandfather was intrigued by this new turn of events.

'If Haabe did have the nerve to show his face anywhere near here, I'm not surprised he ended up in the river!' he said.

'That's all very well,' I objected, 'but if that was the case, why should anyone want to kill me for seeing Haabe's body?'

'You have me there,' agreed Grandfather.

Later, when Duval arrived with the photographs, however, the new theory was disposed of, because I could see no similarity between Haabe and the man in the river.

'His jaw is too square, for one thing,' I decided. 'And the shape of the head is wrong. No. This wasn't the man.'

Duval was disappointed, and I couldn't blame him. He gathered up his photographs, and prepared to take his leave, warning me once again not to go anywhere on my own, and also to let him know what my movements would be if I left Tourloup.

At this point, Monsieur Vincennes called at the office to see if my grandfather and I would be interested in joining a party of his friends who were going to the Casino in Monte Carlo for an hour or so that evening.

'You will have young company, Mademoiselle Mathieson,' he assured me. 'Annemarie will be there, and I intend to ask young Médoc and Monsieur MacIntosh when I see them later today.'

Grandfather looked across at Sergeant Duval to see what he thought of this proposition.

Duval rubbed his chin.

'We can't keep Mademoiselle confined to Tourloup all the time,' he said, 'and I think, provided she sticks close to you all, and you two gentlemen and Monsieur MacIntosh keep a weather eye open for possible "accidents", it should be safe enough for her to go with you.'

'Have you still no idea who or what you are up against?' asked Vincennes gravely.

'Every time I think I have a lead, it finishes at a dead end,' replied the Sergeant. 'It's come to the point where the more I think about it, the more I feel like doubting the evidence which led us to believe these "accidents" were deliberately planned,' he shrugged in disgust. 'The shot fired at Mademoiselle could have been genuine carelessness; the call which took me off to Castellane yesterday a genuine hoax; Monsieur Vincennes was so far from the river he could have been mistaken in what he saw,' – here he held up his hand to stop an angry interruption – 'but I saw where the rock was prised from the ground above the Col. There was no doubt at all it was deliberately moved – and here I tell myself this might have been the work of a madman, aiming for any car and not the particular one in which Miss Mathieson was riding—'

'And you would be wrong,' said Grandfather simply. 'Each factor on its own might point at nothing, but taken together,' he shook his head, 'they all add up to deliberate attempts on the life of one person!'

I felt goose-fleshy all over. Somehow I had found it difficult to imagine that I was the intended victim of a cold-blooded gang, much as in wartime, no soldier, sailor or airman, or civilian for that matter, believes there is a bullet or a bomb with his name on it.

Monsieur Vincennes looked at me sympathetically.

'You must not worry, Mademoiselle Mathieson. Our good Sergeant will soon lay the villains by the heels, even if he has to arrest every stranger who shows his face in Tourloup, eh, Sergeant?'

Duval nodded grimly. 'It may come to that!'

'As for your grandfather and myself,' went on Vincennes. 'Tonight we shall be your bodyguard! You will travel with us, in my car, with Annemarie, but we shall not make the arrangement known until the last minute. Also, coming home, we shall change the guard! You will return in Monsieur MacIntosh's car with Annemarie and young Médoc, but again this will appear to be a last minute decision. What do you say to that, Sergeant?'

'It seems all right,' said Duval cautiously.

'We shall leave here about five-thirty and dine at the Hotel de Paris in Monte Carlo before going on to the Casino. Ça va?'

'What time will you return?'

'Leaving the Casino at eleven, we should be back here, let

me see, by one-thirty. That is not too late for you, Monsieur Verlaine, is it?'

'Beyond my usual bedtime,' acknowledged Grandfather. 'But it is so long since I have been to the Casino, I think it will be worth it!'

Vincennes and Duval left together, and then Grandfather and I went home for lunch.

Martha had prepared Poulet à la Crème for us, according to her favourite recipe. The chicken had been sautéed with onions, poached in water, and served with a cream and egg yolk sauce; it was delicious.

I wondered how our housekeeper could prepare a dish worthy of a cordon bleu, and at the same time, keep my grandfather's villa clean and sparkling.

When we had finished our meal, and I was carrying the dishes back to the kitchen, I complimented her.

'That was a superb lunch!' I told her.

'Ah! But wait until this evening! Then there will be a special treat. A mushroom omelette such as you will never have tasted before!'

'Oh dear!' I exclaimed. 'Hasn't Grandpère told you that we shall be dining out tonight?'

'No one tells me anything!' grumbled Martha. 'The mushrooms will not be fresh enough to use tomorrow. The secret of success in my recipe is cooking with fresh vegetables. None of your deep freeze vegetables for me!'

'Make the omelette for yourself then,' I said brightly.

'You know very well that I am allergic to fungi,' she said crossly.

'Then give them to one of your friends.'

'You could take them to Madame de Jarenté this afternoon,' suggested Martha. 'I am sure she would welcome such a gift.'

'Of course! I never thought of that. I could add some of the vegetables from our own garden.'

'I shall prepare a nice basketful for you,' Martha was delighted because I had agreed with her suggestion. 'Now, out of the kitchen, before you get your pretty dress soiled.'

I almost laughed as I took my leave. Martha's kitchen is so immaculate, I wondered where I would get the dirt from!

Grandfather said he would accompany me to Madame de Jarenté's house and call back for me about half past four.

'That will be a long enough visit, and in any case, you will need time to change before going to Monte Carlo,' he said.

Madame de Jarenté, who had once been a concert pianist of some note, but who was now so crippled with arthritis she was confined permanently to bed, was delighted to see me, and pathetically grateful for the basket of fresh fruit and vegetables and flowers, which I had brought her.

'I do not have many visitors, Lucille,' she said, indicating me to take a chair up beside the bed. 'I am so old, my friends are all dead, and there are many days when I crave to be with them.

'But, alors! That is no way to welcome you!' her pale mouth smiled at me. 'Tell me what you have been doing since you were here last, and yes! let me see your hands. No ring yet?'

I shook my head and hastily steered her off the subject of matrimony.

'I have brought some magazines too. They are at the foot of the basket. Madame Boclus can read them to you later, and you will no doubt laugh together over some of the new fashions!'

Madame Boclus, the old lady's elderly companion, nodded, and taking out the basket I had brought, she left us to talk alone together.

I chatted of my life at the University, of the lectures I went to, and the concerts I had attended that winter.

'Next time I visit you, I shall bring my record player and some of the latest recordings,' I promised. 'I should have thought of that this afternoon.'

'No, my dear. This afternoon it is your voice I wish to listen to,' she assured me. 'Tell me how your grandfather is keeping, and all about the new people who have brought the Villa des Lilas.

'Madame Boclus was complaining because the noise of the

cars going to the party there the other night kept her awake, but I enjoyed the sound. Sometimes it is so quiet here, I feel as if I am already dead, but without the gift of death!'

I described in detail the changes which had taken place in the Villa des Lilas, and I was telling her about Annemarie, and how chic she was, when I noticed the frail head droop in sleep.

I stopped talking and took a look around me.

The room I was in was a large one, but it was difficult to appreciate its size, because so much furniture of the heavy, ornate, old-fashioned kind cluttered it up.

It was even difficult to make out all the bits and pieces because the shutters of the room were half closed to keep the strong daylight from the tired old eyes, and yellowing lace curtains still further dimmed the brightness of the sun which, shortly before lunch, had dispelled the mists and fogs which had veiled Tourloup in the early morning.

The three dominant pieces in the room were the great, high four-poster bed, with its faded hangings and pretty, rose-coloured eiderdown, in which lay the shrunken figure of old Madame de Jarenté; a tall chest of drawers of dark wood, on top of which stood innumerable framed photographs; and most conspicuous of all, a grand piano, whose polished rosewood case reflected the filtered sunlight, and which occupied an entire corner.

I stood up softly and went to have a look at the photographs. I had been shown them all before, but they never failed to fascinate me, especially the ones of the old lady herself taken at the turn of the century, when she had been a beautiful, laughing-eyed girl of twenty, with the world at her feet.

I was standing with this photograph in my hand when there was a gentle tap on the door, and Madame Boclus came in carrying a tray set with cups, coffee pot, and a plate of rich-looking chocolate cake.

'You should not have bothered!' I protested, but the gaunt-faced companion, who looked like a chief mourner in her long black dress and black stockings, with ropes of jet beads pendant from her thin neck and jet ear-rings dangling from her ears, shook her head.

'Eating is the one great pleasure left to her,' she nodded to the figure in the bed. 'The chocolate cake is an afternoon ritual. Only, you must not mind, I shall have to feed her. Poor soul, she can no longer hold even a cake in her crippled hands.'

Madame Boclus gently roused the old lady.

'Your four o'clock, Madame!' she helped Madame de Jarenté to sit up, and plumped the pillows comfortably behind her, and while I poured the coffee, she fed her invalid with mouthfuls of chocolate cake.

I had to turn away to hide the tears in my eyes. To think that this helpless frame still housed the soul and inward fire of the lovely woman who laughed at us from the photograph!

I was glad when the little repast was over and I found myself looking at my watch, and hoping Grandfather would soon call for me.

However, it was only a quarter to four, and after helping Madame Boclus with the dishes, I gratefully accepted her suggestion that I should arrange the flowers I had brought in a vase and place them on the piano.

I had just completed this task when the door-bell rang, and to my surprise, another visitor was shown into the invalid's room.

It was Greg MacIntosh!

'Monsieur MacIntosh!' Madame de Jarenté's voice warmed in welcome. 'How good of you to come and see me again so soon – but see – I have another visitor today!' she proclaimed proudly.

'Lucille,' she went on, after Greg had courteously kissed her twisted fingers, 'this young man's grandfather was an old admirer of mine, or so he says!' she smiled her disbelief. 'Still, it is a pretty tale!'

'And it gives me an excuse to visit you, and keep my hand in on a good piano!' Greg's voice held its usual teasing quality, but it was a quality which obviously delighted his hostess.

'Please play for us, Monsieur. This afternoon I have the strangest longing to hear some of my old favourites – Liszt and Debussy and, yes, Strauss! I should like to hear his waltzes again.'

'You don't mind, do you, Lucille?' asked Greg softly. 'I come over once a week to play for her. It gives pleasure to both of us.

'This afternoon, however, I am killing two birds with one stone, so to speak. I was talking to your grandfather about this proposed visit to Monte Carlo, and he asked if I wouldn't mind accompanying you from here back to the Villa Beau Site, since he would not be able to finish work as early as he had expected.'

Greg sat down at the piano, and for almost an hour he played for the old lady. I sat and listened, amazed at his virtuosity at the keys and when at length he stopped, and said regretfully that it was time for us to go, it took me several seconds to come to after the spell of his music.

There were tears in Madame de Jarenté's eyes as we took our leave.

'You have both made me so happy today,' she put her warped, parchment dry, old hands in ours. 'So very, very happy!'

CHAPTER NINETEEN

We had stayed longer with old Madame de Jarenté than we had intended, and it was going to be a bit of a rush to be ready to leave with Monsieur Vincennes at half past five.

Grandfather had already changed to his evening clothes and was waiting impatiently at the front door when I got out of Greg's car and came running up the path, and while Greg drove away with a curt, 'See you in quarter of an hour,' Grandfather told me to get a move on!

I hurried up to my bedroom, whipped off my scarlet wool

frock, which Martha carefully hung up for me while I showered.

She called out to ask what dress she would lay out for me, and since I didn't want Annemarie to see me in the same thing twice running, I decided against the frock I had worn to her cocktail party, and this meant wearing again the black jersey silk which I had worn the previous evening.

Since I had not time to sweep my hair up into last night's sophisticated style, I hurriedly brushed it out into its usual loose pageboy and let Martha spray it with a star-dust lacquer which brought out its golden highlights.

The only jewellery I put on was a Moorish gold bracelet set with square-cut topazes, and Martha was fastening its safety clasp when the doorbell rang and Grandfather called up that Monsieur Vincennes was waiting for us.

I draped a pastel mink stole – my father's last present to my mother – round my shoulders, and after Martha hurriedly dabbed perfume behind my ears and wrists, I grabbed my evening bag and hurried downstairs.

Monsieur Vincennes' car was a magnificent grey Phantom Rolls Royce, which allowed plenty of room in the back for his daughter to spread out the scarlet brocade skirt of the full length evening dress she was wearing under a fabulous evening jacket of white fox fur. A collar of diamonds and rubies sparkled at her neck, and an ornate diamond comb was stuck Spanish fashion into the coil of her black hair.

She looked so glamorous she made me feel like Cinderella before she went to the ball!

'Have you ever been to the Casino at Monte?' she asked me, once the usual polite good evenings had been exchanged.

I shook my head. 'I have always wanted to go, but somehow, you know how it is, I never quite got round to it.'

'Et vous, Monsieur Verlaine?' she addressed Grandpapa.

'A few times, in my youth, before I was married, but fortunately I never caught the gambling fever, so I did not miss the visits.'

'I prefer taking a calculated business risk to the chance fall of a dice, or the final resting place of an impersonal ball in a spinning wheel,' said Vincennes.

'That is because you are old Papa!' asserted Annemarie. 'The Casino fascinates me! I could spend a lifetime watching the wheel go round and listening to the noise of the chips being raked in!' She sighed. 'I wonder what my luck will be like tonight?'

'I have given you your allowance for a month,' said her father crisply, 'so it had better be good.'

We did not appear to be travelling fast, and yet in no time we reached the main South road. Monsieur Vincennes handled the big car in a way that reminded me of Greg's driving, with mastery and without fuss.

As if she had partly read my mind, Annemarie remarked, somewhat petulantly,

'It is a pity the others are coming in Greg's car and not Raoul's. At the speed he drives, heaven knows when they will arrive!'

'They are right behind us,' replied Vincennes. 'Moreover, the reason I asked Monsieur MacIntosh if he would like to take our friends, the Gautiers, with him is because I felt they would feel a lot safer with him, than with that young Nuvolari of yours!'

Annemarie's lips curled into a pout of annoyance and for the rest of the journey she said nothing.

The other members of Monsieur Vincennes' party were waiting for us in the cocktail bar of the Hotel de Paris, and after a round of introductions, followed by a round of apéritifs, we made our way to our reserved table in the world famous dining-room.

I was partnered by Raoul, who was in an unusually quiet mood, while Greg was being very assiduous in his attentions to Annemarie, a fact which caused me so much unreasonable annoyance, that I went out of my way to flirt lightheartedly with Raoul.

At Monsieur Vincennes' suggestion, after a superb variety of hors d'oeuvres, which was practically a meal in itself, I ordered Piccata des Gourmets Riz Pilaf, a dish for which the hotel is noted, and although I am not a real enthusiast, this dish converted me!

We all finished the meal with Omelette Soufflé Hotel de Paris, and then Monsieur Vincennes said that if we wished to spend any time at all at the Casino, we had better be on our way.

The Casino in Monte Carlo has a very special atmosphere. Compared to modern casinos, it is old-fashioned, but old-fashioned in a splendid way which makes one nostalgic for a past in which princes of royal blood, the old English aristocracy and Russian Grand Dukes lived in a special Ruritania!

Even the present class-levelling of coach parties and conducted tours cannot diminish its grandeur.

It was built in 1878, before the days of the nouveau riche, to the design of the same man, Charles Garnier, who was also responsible for the Opera House in Paris, and it stands as a monument to a society which will never return.

I had to show my passport and get a card before being allowed to enter the palace of gambling, and then I was in the great gilded salon, where drawn curtains shut out the everyday world and the focus of all eyes were the gaming tables with their smooth, green surfaces.

I was so impressed with all I saw, I stared around me, goggle-eyed.

'Lucille, stop behaving like a country cousin,' said Raoul crossly, taking my arm and propelling me after the rest of the party.

At Monte Carlo, trente et quarante and roulette are the favourite games, and it was to the roulette table we were making.

Before leaving for the Casino, I had made up my mind exactly how much I could afford to lose, but Raoul looked down his nose at the amount I gave him to change to chips for me.

'That's chicken feed!' he exclaimed.

'Perhaps to a well paid journalist like you it is!' I retorted angrily, 'but I have only a small living allowance and I know what I can afford to spend on pleasure!'

'Monsieur Vincennes will stake you,' said Raoul. 'He often does that for his friends.'

'I'm no sponger, Raoul. I spend what is mine and I am in debt to no man.'

'Very well,' he sneered, 'but you will only be able to play for a few minutes with those stakes.'

'And that will satisfy me!' I said promptly. 'I am no gambler. I shall get as much pleasure from watching as from playing.'

In this I was quite right. For a while I was so absorbed in watching the players, I placed no stake myself. While Raoul and Annemarie pressed forward to the table, I hovered with my grandfather on the edge of the crowd.

It was fascinating to study the assorted types who were gathered here, and very easy to tell the holidaymakers, who had come in more for the sake of saying they had had a flutter in the famous casino than for anything else, from the veteran gamblers with their poker faces and haunted looking eyes.

Many of the latter had pencils and papers, and Grandfather told me that these were the ones who tried from graphs and charts to work to a system. Gambling to them was more a profession than a game for an idle hour.

All the seats round the table were taken. Someone rose to give way to Annemarie, and she sat down with Raoul standing behind her. Both had stacks of chips in front of them and in both their expressions was a peculiar, almost feverish intensity, and Annemarie's hand was actually trembling as the croupier called out the famous invitation, 'Messieurs. Faîtes vos jeux', and she leaned forward to place her bet on number twenty-one.

I felt so disturbed by her excitement, I could not watch her and I turned my attention to study the roulette wheel.

This wheel consists of a fixed, concave rim, and a converse inner part, which revolves, its edge being divided into thirty-seven compartments, numbered up to thirty-six.

When everyone had placed their bets, 'Rien ne va plus!' called the croupier and set the wheel spinning, almost simultaneously flicking a small ivory ball on the rim in the opposite direction.

All eyes were now on this ball as it danced and jumped about the rim until the spinning wheel stopped to let it come to rest in compartment thirty-five.

Annemarie gave an exclamation of disgust as her money was raked away, but the winner's face was expressionless. An oily looking Middle Eastern national rubbed his damp forehead with an immaculate white handkerchief; an old woman, with face so raddled with wrinkles that the paint and powder on her cheeks cracked in a thousand lines, marked off a note in the little book she consulted; Raoul whispered into Annemarie's ear, and once again, at the croupier's invitation, she placed an even bigger stake on her original number.

After she and Raoul, who seemed to be playing in combination, had lost for the fifth time, Monsieur Vincennes managed to get a seat for me at the table.

Rather hesitantly, I placed a quarter of my chips on number three. I lost, but Grandfather was in luck. With legal caution, he collected his winnings and went to change his chips, deciding it was a good idea to cash in on a winning streak, and thereafter he was merely a spectator.

After four shots I had lost all my chips, so I decided to call it a day. Monsieur Vincennes and his friends played on for modest stakes, but not so Annemarie and Raoul.

Although I reckoned that already they had lost a considerable sum, they kept doubling up on the same number. Monsieur Vincennes shot his daughter a worried look and signalled her to stop, but she was lost to the gambling urge. Watching her, I felt myself grow quite hot with worrying for her, until at last I could stand the suspense no longer, and I made my way out of the gaming room to the terrace, where the floodlighting made the blossoms of the trailing geranium plants seem unnaturally scarlet.

I stood alone looking out across the bay, watching the myriad lights of the launches and steam yachts of the rich bobbing up and down in the harbour, listening to the faint strains of music from a distant orchestra, inhaling the clean sweet air which was blown inland from the Mediterranean and wishing, wistfully, that I could turn back the clock so that the threat of sudden death which loomed over me was not real; that Raoul was still a gay adolescent and not an ambitious man of the world: that Jules Lamartine was not ill, so that I could visit him and listen to his stories of old country days and ways: and above all, that there was not a glamorous woman like Annemarie Cordet to distract the attention of Greg MacIntosh.

Here my wishful thinking ceased, because if this past week were to be wiped from the slate of time, there would be no Greg MacIntosh in my life, and as I stood there, leaning against the stone balustrade, with the evening breeze softly brushing my long hair across my shoulders, I faced the fact that the reason I disliked Annemarie so; the reason why my heart beat erratically when I saw him; the reason I acted so perversely in his company, was because I had fallen in love with the teasing, annoying, but oh, so very attractive young engineer.

I flushed with shame at my weakness. How typical of me to fall in love with a man who was in love with someone else, and who saw me almost in the capacity of an exasperating young sister!

Now that I had admitted my feelings to myself I felt I should never be able to face Greg again. The best thing for me to do was to get back to Edinburgh and stay there, until I got over this senseless infatuation. I might even be able to persuade Grandfather to return with me for a week or two, so that he could be present at the graduation ceremony, and so that I could show him round the city his daughter had grown to love.

I heard a whisper of footsteps on the terrace behind me, but I was not in the mood for company and I quickly moved away and stood, as I hoped, out of sight behind the long fronds of a potted palm tree.

However, my luck was out. The palm leaves were pulled aside with a swift, jerky movement, which stirred up an elusive memory and Raoul, his face bleached of colour by the overhead lighting, stood staring at me.

'So this is where you have got to!' he said. 'I was looking all over for you.'

He moved so close to me that the sleeve of his dinner jacket brushed against my arm.

'You look sad, Lucille. You weren't contemplating running away and throwing yourself in the harbour after your crippling loss at the table?'

'Don't be silly,' I said crossly. 'I came out here because it was so hot and stuffy inside, and I couldn't bear the atmosphere of despair and hope and – and money greed!' I gave a little shiver. 'Some of these people looked as if they would trade their souls with the devil, if it would make them win!'

Raoul laughed harshly as he pushed aside a frond which was brushing against his ear.

'What would you know of the devil, Lucille? You are as innocent as the cherubs in the Cathedral of the Immaculate Virgin there,' he pointed vaguely. 'You—' he stopped.

'Why are you looking at me like that?' he asked with a frown.

'It is your hands, Raoul. The way you parted the leaves just now almost made me remember something which was niggling me.' I wrinkled my brow thoughtfully.

'I wish it would come back to me! I am sure it is something important! Oh! it is too aggravating! Hands, Raoul, hands! Tell me, what is there important about hands?' I looked up at him.

Raoul was now standing with his back to the light and I couldn't make out the expression on his face, but unexpectedly he gripped my arm, forcing me back against the balustrade and almost over it.

I was so taken aback at this sudden, unlooked for display of passion that I let out a startled scream.

'No! Raoul! No!' I tried to struggle free.

Next moment, to my mingled chagrin and relief, Greg MacIntosh loomed up behind Raoul, and he said, coldly.

'Lucille, your grandfather is waiting for you. He and

Monsieur Vincennes feel it is time we set off for home.'

Raoul let go of me, and stalked off giving Greg a disconcerted look, while I put a hand unsteadily to my hair to sweep it back from my face. With the movement I became conscious of an aching pain in my upper arms from the violence of Raoul's grip.

Greg was looking at me oddly and I felt so self-conscious I turned away to retrieve my stole, which had fallen into the palm tub when Raoul had seized me, and I took my time about picking it up, glad of an excuse to hide my flaming cheeks from Greg's gaze.

Annoyed by the interruption, Raoul had stalked off ahead of us, so that it was Greg who courteously helped me to drape the wrap round my shoulders and at the electric touch of his fingers on my shoulders, I shivered suddenly.

'Come away from here before you catch a chill,' he said brusquely, taking my arm and escorting me to where the rest of the party were waiting for us.

Raoul and Annemarie wanted to go on to a night-club to round off the evening, but her father was firm with her.

'Other people have to work tomorrow, ma chère,' he said. 'Not everyone can afford to play all night.'

With that, he shook hands with those of his guests who had joined the party at the Hotel de Paris, and when they had all gone, he remarked casually he thought that the young ones, by which he meant Annemarie, Raoul, Greg and myself, should go home together and he would take Grandfather and the Gautiers.

Raoul still seemed displeased at being interrupted in his amorous scene in the garden, and as if to pay me back for what, after all, had not been my fault, he turned his attentions to Annemarie, cajoled her into sitting in the back seat of the car with him, and ignored me completely.

Greg looked as if he didn't appreciate this arrangement, but there wasn't much he could do about it, so he told me to get into the front seat beside him and, after that, not a word passed between us.

I felt sorrow for both of us, especially as Annemarie paid no attention to him either, and instead sat snuggled in Raoul's arm, with her head resting on his shoulder.

CHAPTER TWENTY

The drive back to Tourloup seemed interminable. Greg sat grimly silent, concentrating on his driving and ignoring both me and the occupants of the back seat. The only break in the monotony was when we overtook Vincennes' Rolls Royce on the road north, were passed by it a few miles before we branched off for Tourloup and then once more we took the lead just before the road narrowed at the Col.

'Are you playing races?' I raised my brows as we took the lead once more.

Greg's eyes met my glance in the driving mirror.

He shook his head. 'Merely being cautious,' he said in a low voice, which would not carry to the passengers behind us, but I doubt if Raoul or Annemarie would have heard him, even if he had shouted the words, they were so absorbed with each other.

I felt myself go cold all over. 'I had forgotten about that.'

Greg's hands tightened on the steering wheel.

'No doubt at the moment you have other things on your mind,' and this time the glimpse in the mirror was at the two seated behind him.

At first I didn't grasp what he meant, but then he added, kindly, 'Annemarie is only flirting with Raoul, Lucille. He will soon come to his senses,' and I realized that he thought I was looking glum because Raoul was playing the fool with Madame Cordet, and because, living in Tourloup, he was bound to have heard some of the local gossip which linked our names romantically together.

I opened my mouth to tell him that even the friendly feeling I had had for Raoul in the past had become diluted of recent months, but almost immediately I changed my mind.

Why should I tell Greg I no longer cared for Raoul? The affair of my heart would be of no interest to him, and he might even ask, jokingly, if there was someone else, and how could I answer that?

We arrived at Tourloup and Greg drove right through the village to the last house on the far outskirts, which was the Médocs. Here, with obvious reluctance, Raoul had to leave us.

The Villa Beau Site is only about a couple of hundred feet or so from the Médocs, and by the time Raoul had bidden Annemarie a series of fond farewells, we saw Vincennes' Rolls Royce stop outside our house and Grandfather got out.

Greg turned his car and drew up behind the Rolls and, at the bidding of her father, Annemarie stepped from the Alfa and went to join her father who, after wishing us all good night, reversed his car into our entrance, turned and went swiftly back down the High Street.

Greg followed Grandfather and me into our house, where both men had a quick look round to ensure all was in order, and then Greg took his leave and Grandfather carefully locked and bolted the front door after him.

I went to bed, but it was a long time before I fell asleep.

I lay thinking of the curious tangle human relationships can get into. I had fallen in love with Greg, but neither he nor Raoul Médoc could see another woman because they were both bewitched by the lovely Annemarie.

As for Annemarie, whether she was in love with Raoul or Greg, or neither, I could not tell, but she was certainly an adept at keeping her men on tenterhooks, and as I thought of how she played one off against the other, I decided that if this was how the game of love was played, I wanted no part of it and the sooner I tried to get my infatuation for Greg MacIntosh out of my system, the better.

On this resolve, I must have fallen asleep, for when next I opened my eyes, instead of silvery moonlight penetrating the shutter slats, golden sunshine was pouring through the open window, and Martha was neatly hanging up the dress I had forgotten to put away the night before.

'Bonjour, Martha,' I struggled up to a sitting position. 'What time is it, please?'

'Almost mid-day, ma petite. I came to waken you at breakfast time, but you were sleeping so soundly, your grandfather said not to disturb you.'

'Oh, dear!' I said guiltily. 'I was supposed to help him in the office again this morning, because he gave Mimi the day off.'

'Your grandfather has got on without Mimi before,' said Martha comfortingly, 'but he did say he would expect you to make up for lost time this afternoon!' She shook her head. 'The way he fusses about you these days, you would think he was afraid to let you out of his sight. Why!' she raised her shoulders, 'he even told me I was not to leave the house to do my shopping until you were awake!'

'He is worse than a mother hen, isn't he?' I said lightly, and to change the subject, since it had been agreed that Martha was not to know of the danger I was in, I said, 'What do you think I should put on today? I can hardly wear denim jeans to a lawyer's office!'

'I have cleaned and pressed the skirt you wore on the day you arrived,' said Martha. 'I am sure that it and this white piqué blouse would be most suitable.'

'Good! Then I shall shower and dress.'

'By which time I shall prepare you a cup of hot chocolate. Nothing to eat, though,' she said firmly. 'It is much too near the hour of déjeuner for that.'

I went to the bathroom for a shower and when I had dressed and come downstairs, Martha was standing in the back yard, talking to the daily woman who cleaned the Médocs' villa.

Both women looked upset as they chattered away ten to the dozen. Eventually, the daily hurried off, Martha returned to her kitchen and then came out to the terrace, carrying my cup of chocolate, and looking most distressed.

'Ma petite, I have shocking news for you,' she said.

I started. 'What has happened?'

'Madame de Jarenté is dead!' blurted out Martha. 'The poor old soul!'

'Dead!' I couldn't believe it. 'She seemed all right when we left her yesterday afternoon. In fact, she was looking unusually well!'

'She took ill during the night, Madame Boclus too!'

'What!' I exclaimed. 'Don't tell me she is dead too!'

'Non, non! She is not dead, but she is very, very ill. It seems it was something they ate.'

'Oh, Bon Dieu!' I said aghast. 'How awful! Do you know what it was?'

'I understand it was some kind of stew they had for supper. Dr. Médoc is having the remains analysed, or so I was told.'

'Poor Madame de Jarenté!' tears filled my eyes. 'To die like that.'

I left my cup of chocolate untasted and stared out unhappily across the terrace. I was still sitting there when Grandfather came home for lunch.

He, too, had heard of the old pianist's death, and was much grieved by it.

'We can only pray that poor Madame Boclus recovers. She is still very ill and has not been told of her employer's death.'

We picked at our lunch in melancholy silence, until Grandfather spotted Doctor Médoc's car coming up the road.

'I must ask him how Madame Boclus is,' he said, rising to his feet and pushing back his chair. 'You know, there have been so many tragedies here of late, one would almost think the village accursed!'

He hurried from the dining-room and reached the garden gate in time to wave the doctor to a standstill, and a few seconds later, both men entered the house.

Médoc looked so ill himself, I wondered how he could spare the energy to attend to his patients. There were deep, dark hollows under his eyes, and he seemed to have shrunk since last I saw him.

'Madame Boclus has just died,' Grandfather informed me sombrely.

'Bon Dieu!' I shivered. 'There is a jinx over all of us!'

'Have you discovered the cause of the deaths?' Grandfather demanded. 'I heard it was something they ate.'

Médoc nodded wearily. 'There were mushrooms in the stew they had for supper and somehow a few deadly ones had been mixed with them.'

I started so violently that both men looked at me.

'Mushrooms!' I exclaimed, 'Mushrooms! Bon Dieu! Bon Dieu!' I looked at Grandfather with anguished eyes.

'Do you think it could have been the ones I took to them yesterday afternoon?'

Doctor Médoc looked at me with his unhappy eyes.

'Did you take mushrooms to Madame de Jarenté yesterday?' he asked, very slowly.

I nodded.

'Martha had got some to make one of her special omelettes for supper, but since we were going out, and since she is allergic to them, I took them along with some other vegetables as a gift to Madame de Jarenté.'

'Where did Martha get the vegetables? At the market?' asked Grandfather, perturbed.

'I don't know.'

'We must ask her,' said Médoc harshly. 'I want no more deaths on my hands. I have had enough!'

I went to the kitchen and told the housekeeper that Doctor Médoc wished to have a word with her.

'Martha,' he fixed her with his deep-set eyes. 'These mushrooms you gave to Lucille to take to Madame de Jarenté, where did you buy them?'

'Buy them?' echoed Martha. 'I didn't buy them. Someone left a basket of them at the door. I thought at first they were from old Lamartine. He often used to leave them, but of course, he's ill just now—'

'Someone left them at the door, you say?' Doctor Médoc interrupted her. 'Did you see who it was?'

I looked at him anxiously. His face, pale enough before,

was now ashen and beads of perspiration oozed from the pores of his forehead.

Martha shook her head.

'Bon Dieu!' whispered Grandfather, looking at me. 'Lucille, those mushrooms were meant for you!'

Martha looked from one to other of us in consternation.

'What is it all about?' she asked puzzled.

'Madame de Jarenté and Madame Boclus are both dead from eating poisonous mushrooms!' I said in horror. 'It might have been Monsieur Verlaine and myself, if we hadn't been so generous,' I said bitterly. 'We are responsible for their deaths!'

'No! You mustn't say that!' Doctor Médoc spoke angrily. 'It was an accident. An accident,' he repeated wiping his perspiring brow. 'It must have been a gift from some child who did not know the different fungi,' he spoke half to himself. 'Yes, that's what it would be!' and without even bidding us good-bye, he stalked to the door, let himself out and hurried to his car.

'That poor man should be in bed,' said Martha. 'He looks ready to collapse.'

'He takes too much on himself,' said Grandfather. 'He looks after the health of the entire community single-handed, and we had a lot of illness for him to attend to this winter – to say nothing of the time taken up dancing attendance on a selfish wife—'

'And nursing old Jules, too!' I put in. 'Grandpère, couldn't you talk some sense into him?'

'I'll have a word with Raoul,' he said decisively. 'In fact, I shall telephone him right now!'

Martha took away the remains of our luncheon, which had grown cold and unpalatable.

'To think that you and your grandfather might have eaten those horrible things!' she muttered to me. 'Never again, do you hear, never again, shall I have a mushroom in the house!' and still muttering she retired to the kitchen.

Grandfather came back from the phone. 'Raoul wasn't in,' he said, 'and there was no point in saying anything to

Madame Médoc,' he added in disgust. 'She wouldn't have paid any attention to me.'

'You realize, Grandfather, that these mushrooms which caused the deaths of the old ladies weren't left by accident, as Doctor Médoc appeared to think. They were meant for me!'

I was more angry than alarmed. 'Don't you think we should get in touch with Sergeant Duval and tell him about this?'

Grandfather seemed hardly aware that I had spoken.

'This afternoon, Lucille, I am going to ask Monsieur MacIntosh to drive you to Nice airport and put you on the first flight for London, and you will then fly not to Edinburgh, but to Glasgow, to stay with friends there. I am also going to ask Sergeant Duval to apply for assistance in this case. He cannot handle this evil on his own!'

'But—'

'No buts, Lucille, I am frightened. More frightened than I ever was, even in the darkest hours under the Nazis. We are up against someone ruthless. Someone who does not care how many people are involved in his attacks on you! The other day, Monsieur MacIntosh could have been killed with you.'

I started.

Grandfather went on, 'Yesterday he did not care if Martha and I were also victims of his vendetta. No,' he shook his head, 'we must get you away from here safely, without anyone knowing your ultimate destination.'

He paced up and down the room.

'First, you will dress as if for a day at the beach, but you will fill your beachbag with the essentials you need for a journey. I shall take your travel costume and shoes to the office in my briefcase, and hand them to Monsieur MacIntosh when he calls. All other clothes you can buy when you arrive in Scotland.' He nodded. 'Of course, you will no doubt still have a lot of clothes in your flat in Edinburgh, so the expense should not be too great.'

'It's impossible!' I protested. 'I can't run away like that.'

'Doing the sensible thing is not the same as being a

coward, my child. It would make life easier for me, and also for your friends, if you left here.'

'No!' I denied this. 'You said before I might be in danger wherever I went, and I think the best thing I could do is to stay on here, and act as bait! Then I would feel I was doing something to avenge the deaths of these innocent old women.'

Back and forward we argued, each of us getting more and more exasperated with the other, and we were still both sticking stubbornly to our own point of view, when the door-bell rang and Martha announced the arrival of Sergeant Duval.

'The very man we were wanting to see!' Grandfather greeted him. 'We should like to discuss with you the deaths of Madame de Jarenté and Madame Boclus,' he went on.

'What about them?' asked Duval sharply.

'Dr Médoc has no doubt told you that these two unfortunates died as the result of eating poisonous mushrooms?'

The Sergeant nodded.

'But did he also tell you, Sergeant, that these mushrooms were intended not for the de Jarenté household, but for the Villa Beau Site?'

'Zut!' The Sergeant whistled through his teeth. 'How so?'

Grandfather explained.

'Bon Dieu!' Duval looked at us with startled eyes. 'And your good Martha has no idea who left the basket at your door?'

We shook our heads.

'That is why I am sending Lucille away from here,' said Grandfather. 'She must run no more risks!'

'No! I am not leaving!' I interrupted firmly.

My grandfather ignored me. 'It is also why, Sergeant Duval, I now beg of you to get outside help. Something evil is going on here in Tourloup, and we need all the help we can to put an end to it.'

'There is a curse on this place!' Duval repeated my grandfather's earlier utterance. 'And it all seemed to start with the drowned man.'

He glared at me, as if it was all my fault. I was about to retort that I wasn't any happier about the position than he was, when there was another ring at the doorbell, and seconds later the Sergeant's young aide was shown into the room.

'It's Doctor Médoc,' he said without preamble. 'He's dead!'

CHAPTER TWENTY-ONE

There was a moment of shocked silence, and then Duval spoke harshly,

'What do you mean?'

'Doctor Médoc is dead,' repeated the white-faced policeman. 'When I went to his house, as you had ordered, to ask for a written report on the deaths of the old ladies, Madame Médoc told me he had not come home yet.

'As I was leaving, I spotted his car in the garage and he was sitting at the wheel. I went over to speak to him,' the policeman gulped. 'He was slumped forward and at first I thought he had fallen asleep. I tapped on the window, but he didn't move, and then – then' – he drew a deep breath – 'I saw a hypodermic syringe beside him on the seat, and a note.'

'Yes?' barked the Sergeant, loud mouthed from tension.

'I opened the door, Sergeant. I felt for his pulse, but could detect no beat. I even held a mirror to his mouth, but there were no signs of clouding. He was dead, although death must only have occurred very recently, for the body was still warm and limp.'

'The note, man. The note!' demanded Duval. 'What did it say?'

'I have it here,' the policeman handed a scrap of paper to his superior.

'I can't go on,' read Duval, 'I have not the heart.'

The numbness which had paralysed me after the policeman's first shocking words, had worn off.

'Suicide!' I whispered. 'The poor, poor man!'

'He hadn't looked himself for days,' Grandfather said sadly. 'Ill-health, over-work, a demanding wife and a son whose extravagance worried him, all these things dragged him down, and on top of that, there was this morning's ghastly tragedy. It must all have combined to make him despair – but surely – surely he could have turned to one of us!' he burst out angrily. 'If I had known what was in his mind when he left here – I might have saved him!'

'You don't suppose Médoc's death is connected in any way with the other business?' said Duval tentatively.

'You mean those attacks on Lucille?' Grandfather stared at him in astonishment. 'Of course not! He was very fond of Lucille! Everyone knows he would have liked her as a daughter-in-law. And not only that, wasn't he the one who diagnosed mushroom poisoning as the cause of the old ladies' deaths? He surely wouldn't have drawn attention to the fact if he had intended to do away with Lucille by that means.'

'He wasn't to know where the mushrooms the women ate came from,' said Duval stubbornly. 'And he was quick at diagnosing the source of the poison!'

'Rubbish!' said Grandfather. 'You are merely looking for an easy solution to your problem.'

'I haven't told Madame Médoc that her husband is dead,' put in the policeman timidly. 'I thought I'd come straight to you and tell you about it, Sergeant.'

'Madame Médoc doesn't know!' ejaculated the Sergeant.

He looked hopefully at Grandpère.

'You are an old friend of the family,' he said. 'You might be able to break the news more gently.'

'Such news can never be broken gently,' said Grandfather bleakly, 'but if you wish it, I shall come with you to the Médoc villa, and Lucille,' he turned to me, 'perhaps you would be so kind as to come with us. Another woman can be a help at a time like this.'

'How about Raoul? Shouldn't he be contacted?'

'Raoul was not at home when I telephoned less than half an hour ago,' said Grandfather, 'and his mother did not know where he was.'

'No doubt he is with Madame Cordet,' I said. 'Shall I telephone the Villa des Lilas?'

'I'll do that,' said Duval. 'I don't mind dealing with a man in a situation like this, but a woman – ah, non!'

Even as we were speaking a car stopped outside the front gate.

'Talk of the devil!' exclaimed Duval as we recognized the scarlet Mercedes. 'Young Médoc himself!'

Raoul got out of his car and came hurrying up the path. Before he reached the front door, Duval went out to meet him.

'Is there something wrong here?' I heard Raoul ask. 'When I saw the police car outside, I was worried.'

I wasn't very sure if I should go out to him when Duval broke the news, but Grandfather motioned me to wait.

'I am afraid we have bad news for you, Monsieur Médoc,' said Duval gravely.

'Not Lucille!' exclaimed Raoul.

'Ah, non! Pas Mademoiselle Mathieson,' said Duval, leading him into the house. 'It concerns your father.'

'Father!' Raoul went so white I thought he would faint. 'Father!' he repeated shakily. 'What has he been up to?'

'Your father is dead,' said Duval simply.

'Raoul, come here and sit down, my lad,' said Grandpère kindly. 'Sergeant Duval will explain. Lucille,' he beckoned me, 'some cognac, if you please.'

I filled a glass and hovered helplessly outside the group of men while Raoul was told of his family's tragedy.

He sat still for a long time, twisting the crystal glass of cognac round and round between his fingers.

'He lacked stamina,' he said at last, his lips twisting in

what, in other circumstances, I would have said was a sneer. 'Yes. He always lacked moral fibre!'

Grandfather shot Raoul a puzzled look.

'Your father was not a well man, Raoul,' he said rather curtly. 'A man only takes his own life when he is too tired, or too upset, to think things out sanely.'

'How did Maman take the news?'

'She hasn't been told yet,' said Duval quickly. 'We thought you should tell her.'

'Yes,' Raoul rose to his feet. 'That would be best.'

'I'll come with you, if you like, Raoul,' I offered. 'Your mother might like to have another woman in the house at a time like this.'

'You!' Raoul stared at me as if he thought I had said something downright stupid. 'My mother would not want you at a time like this,' and with that he put down his empty glass and strode from the room, leaving the police to follow after.

I flushed both at his tone and the rudeness of his action.

'You must make allowances, Lucille. Poor Raoul is not himself,' said Grandfather sympathetically. 'You stay here with Martha and I'll go along with the men and see if there is anything I can do.'

I watched them all leave, Grandfather going in the red Mercedes with Raoul, while the police followed in their own car, and then I wandered restlessly round the house, giving Martha a hand in the kitchen, rearranging the flowers in their vases, and all the time wondering what effect Doctor Médoc's sudden death would have on the community.

One thing was certain, as things had worked out, there would be no question of my going to Nice airport with Greg this afternoon.

Grandfather returned from the doctor's house about twenty minutes later.

'Madame Médoc was wonderful, wonderful,' he said with admiration. 'She took the news quite calmly. I was truly surprised at her good sense.'

'And what now?' I asked.

Grandfather glanced at his watch.

'I shall have to go straight to the office. There is a lot of work to be attended to, and I don't know when I shall be back. Tell Martha not to prepare supper until eight o'clock at least.'

Without a mention of our previous discussion, he took his briefcase and hurried off, and I was left wondering how to fill in the rest of the afternoon.

I picked a book from the library shelf and went out to the terrace, but I couldn't settle to read.

After a time, Martha came out to tell me we had run short of milk and she would have to go to the dairy for some. Knowing Martha, I guessed this was merely an excuse for her to go out and have a gossip with her friends about all the excitement of the day, so I told her there was no need to hurry back, because Grandfather would not be home until almost eight o'clock.

As I watched her leave the house, carrying the milk pitcher. I remembered something which made me start to my feet.

Jules Lamartine!

With Doctor Médoc's death, there would now be no one to go up to the shack on the hillside and attend to the old man. Why! In the general excitement he might be left on his own for days, with no one to bring him food, tend to his needs, or milk his goats.

Without thinking beyond the moment, I ran to the kitchen, picked up a basket and placed in it some bread and cheese, a length of home-made sausage, and some fresh fruit. I filled a vacuum flask with soup which I ladled from the simmering pot on the range, and as an afterthought, added a bottle of vin ordinaire to the pile.

I was pulling on a jacket when the telephone rang.

It was Greg.

My heart beat in double quick time when I recognized his voice, and I told myself off for being such a fool.

'I met Monsieur Verlaine on the way to his office, Lucille,' he said. 'He was asking me if I would take you to the coast tomorrow.'

'I thought he had forgotten about that!' I said in disgust.

'And I think he is quite right!' retorted Greg firmly. 'After what happened today—' he broke off abruptly. 'Lucille, you would be a fool to stay on in Tourloup under the circumstances.'

'Everyone seems anxious to be rid of me, one way or the other!' I said half jokingly. 'I seem to be the great unwanted!'

'Don't be a silly goose!' Greg growled. 'You are a very popular young woman in Tourloup. Everyone has a good word for you. You should hear how Monsieur Vincennes sings your praises.'

'An old man's darling!' I laughed. 'And talking of old men – Martha happened to say we were short of milk, and that reminded me of Jules Lamartine. With Médoc dead, there is no one to milk his goats.'

'Don't you go off there on your own!' said Greg sternly.

'Oh. It's Martha who is going for the milk,' I prevaricated.

'Does that mean you are on your own now?' Greg sounded most concerned about my welfare, and this pleased me. Perhaps, after all, he did like me, a little.

'I'm quite able to look after myself,' I told him.

'Don't open the door to strangers while she is gone,' he ignored my interruption. 'She won't be long, will she?'

'The dairy is not very far away.' Again the truth conveyed the wrong meaning.

'Then look after yourself, Lucille. I have to ring off now.'

I stood holding on to the telephone for several seconds after Greg had rung off, as if by doing so I could still feel myself in communication with him, and then, laughing wryly at my wishful thinking, I replaced the instrument, picked up the basket I had packed for Jules, and left the house.

The only dwelling house between the Villa Beau Site and the path which led up the old glacier to Lamartine's shack was the Médoc's, so I felt reasonably safe in the knowledge that no strangers would spot me as I hurried on my way.

All the shutters of the Médoc villa were closed, giving the place an empty, soulless quality, and I wondered how long it would be before Madame Médoc persuaded her son to take her to Paris with him, shutting up the house until a suitable buyer turned up.

The trail to Jules' little wooden home was steep and I was quite breathless by the time I approached it.

A finger of smoke came from the chimney, indicating that at least the stove was going, and I wondered if there were enough logs cut to keep the fire on until Jules was fit to gather wood for himself.

The goats tethered to the tree outside the hut looked up as I approached, and then resumed feeding on what greenery they could reach. They did not appear to be in need of milking and I wondered if perhaps poor Doctor Médoc had been up to see his old patient that morning, in spite of the village tragedy, or else if Jules himself was so much better he had managed to tend to his animals himself.

My rubber-soled walking shoes made no noise on the ground as I walked towards the cottage door. I lifted my hand to knock, but at that very moment, the door was opened, and I do not know who gave the greatest start – me or the man with the grey beard who had opened the door.

Greybeard recovered first. His strong, wiry hands closed round my wrist, and I was dragged roughly into the hut while he kicked the door closed behind us. Then I was propelled violently across the room, so that the provisions in my basket jumped out and scattered across the floor.

As I tripped over a stool and went sprawling on my knees, fear such as I had never before experienced tied my tongue, so that I could not even scream for help, for the man who was looking at me with murder in his eyes was not Jules Lamartine, but a stranger!

CHAPTER TWENTY-TWO

'You are not Jules!' I found my voice at last.

The man laughed, a dry, unamused laugh.

'No. I am not Jules. That is why I discouraged people from visiting me here.'

He stood over me, eyes narrowed. 'But now that you are here, I have to decide what is to be done about you.'

He seized me by the wrist, pulled me to my feet, and twisting my arm viciously behind my back, so that I let out a scream of pain, he forced me into the little room at the back of the shack, which had been Jules' bedroom.

With his free hand, he grabbed a narrow leather belt from the chair beside the bed, and before I could appreciate what he intended to do he had secured my hands tightly behind my back with it, and finally strapped them firmly to the iron bed post.

'Help!' I shouted. 'A moi!' But my screams only served to amuse my captor.

'No one will hear you up here,' he said. 'For nowadays no one comes to visit poor Jules!'

'You fiend!' I raged. 'Who are you? What are you up to? And where is Jules?' My voice rose, 'Where is Jules? What have you done to him?'

Calmly, the man removed his long, false grey beard.

'This served as an excellent disguise. And this,' he removed a wig of long, white hair. 'Poor Jules didn't need these any more, and I saw their usefulness to me!'

'No!' I cringed against the bed post. 'You couldn't! You didn't kill the old man!'

'Lamartine got in my way,' said the stranger in his harsh, peculiarly accented voice. 'He saw me one night digging in the castle ruins, and recognized me, which was too bad for him. He had to be killed!'

I stared aghast at the merciless face in front of mine, noting the too-pale eyes, the close-cropped hair, the ears as pointed as a satyr's, and the bullet-shaped line of head, and slowly the realization dawned.

'You are Heinrich Haabe!' I exclaimed. 'The German garrison commander!'

He gave me a mocking bow.

'I had the feeling you were on the verge of recognizing me, the last time you came to the hut. That was why I felt you had to be got rid of.'

'How could I recognize you? All I saw was a bearded face against the window. Naturally, I assumed it was Jules.'

'You assumed it, yes, but I could see that something puzzled you. I watched from behind the curtains as you walked reluctantly away. At one point you hesitated, and made as if to come back. Yes! You had realized there was something wrong, but what?'

'Of course!' I bit my lip in vexation as the thought which had puzzled me on and off since my visit to Jules came clearly to my mind. 'To think I failed to appreciate it! How could I!'

I stared at him, horrified at the recollection which had come too late to save other lives than mine.

'Bon Dieu!' I muttered. 'How blind can one be! It was your hands I noticed! Your fine, strong fingered hands, as they closed the curtains to hide you from my view. I vaguely noticed them, but I was so upset at what I had thought was a dear friend's rudeness, that the fact that they were not weak and mutilated did not properly register! But I would have remembered in time. I kept trying to think what it was that had bothered me.'

'That was what I was afraid of,' said the Major. 'I knew I had done something wrong, something out of character, and I didn't want you to stir up another investigation!'

'But Jules – where is he? Where did you bury him?'

Haabe gave me a cruel, mocking gaze.

'I made a mistake there. Another mistake which you unfortunately stumbled on. You see, Fraülein, the floods at the week-end washed him from his shallow grave by the river, and—'

'No!' Tears welled from my eyes, and coursed down my cheeks. 'Was it Jules that I found in the water meadow?'

Haabe nodded. 'You very nearly recognized him, too, and then the game would have been up with a vengeance. Fortunately for me, however, you had never seen him without his long grey beard and flowing hair, or your recognition would have been immediate, but if the police you called on had found the body, someone would have identified him! That was why I had to lay the false scarecrow trail, to give me time to recover his body myself and bury it elsewhere!'

'You are inhuman!' I gasped.

'Inhuman?' He appeared surprised at my choice of words. 'I was merely guarding my own interests. I spent the twenty best years of my life locked up, away from the world; from good food; from good wine; from women; and I determined when I got out, I would enjoy life to the full, with the proceeds of the Mercredi treasure, which I knew was buried in a secret vault under the ruins of their castle. No one is going to deprive me of this! Not Jules. Not you. No one!'

'You will never get away with it!' I bit my lips to keep them from quivering. 'My friends will be looking for me, and they know where to look! You have no one to help you – no one!'

There was a knock at the door.

Immediately I let out a piercing scream for help.

Haabe jumped, and whipped me across the face, full force, with the back of his hand, shocking me to silence.

I heard the front door being flung open and a voice called out, 'What's going on? Can I come in?'

My heart lifted with hope. Viciously I bit into the hand that was trying to gag me.

'Raoul!' I screamed. 'Be careful! I am a prisoner! A madman . . .' my voice trailed away as Raoul walked into the bedroom, looked at me for a brief moment, not with the eyes of a friend, but with the same cold, pitiless gaze which Haabe was also directing at me!

Completely ignoring my plea, he turned to the German.

'I happened to see her walking in this direction and, as soon as I could, I came to see if you needed any help.'

'Raoul!' I couldn't believe my ears. 'Raoul! You don't understand! You must help me. This man means to kill me!'

Haabe laughed.

'You needn't expect any help from Rudi,' he used the German equivalent of Raoul. 'On the contrary,' he went on, with a sneer, 'he is as interested in disposing of you as I am!'

'It would be best to wait until it is dark, before we do anything,' said Raoul, still ignoring me. 'We don't want anyone to think there is anything odd going on here, and if Lucille came to see Jules, others might do the same.'

'Raoul!' I made a final plea. 'How can you treat me like this? You loved me once!'

'And you rejected that love!' he turned on me. 'I wasn't good enough for you, that was it, wasn't it? My father was—' he stopped abruptly.

'Your father is dead!' I cried. 'Hardly cold, and you can behave like this. Have you no shame?'

'Médoc? Dead?' Haabe interrupted me. 'When did this happen?'

'An hour, two hours ago,' Raoul informed him. 'I told you he would break! The deaths of the two old women proved too much for him, and he killed himself.'

'What are you talking about? What two women died?'

'Your gift of poisonous mushrooms to the Villa Beau Site was diverted to another household,' Raoul informed him. 'There they proved how effective they would have been!'

'You sent us the mushrooms?' I stared, horrified, at Haabe. 'You would stop at nothing! Not even killing innocents! You are a fiend! As for you, Raoul – you have gone mad! Your father—'

'If you are referring to the unfortunate Médoc,' Raoul mocked me. 'You are mistaken in calling him my father.'

'Rudi is my son,' announced Haabe with pride.

I thought my mind was beginning to go.

'Yes,' continued the Major, 'Madame Médoc and I had a very happy liaison while I was commandant here. Of course,' he smiled coldly, 'we were very discreet and clever! Everyone thought it was the apothecary's wife I was interested in!'

'Then it was not her, but Madame Médoc who betrayed the Mercredis!' I gasped.

Haabe bowed. 'Yes. She betrayed them, not only for love of me, but because she hated them. They treated her like dirt, because she refused to co-operate with them. They thought she lacked backbone!' He sneered. 'But it was the Mercredis who were weak. The Count tried to buy the lives of his wife and daughter-in-law and her children, by offering to tell me where the family fortune was hidden. He had actually started to tell me how to reach the secret vault, when his wife screamed to him to be silent. She was wiser than he, for she realized once the secret was told, their safeguard was gone!'

'You would have killed them in any case,' I looked at him in loathing. 'You enjoy taking life! It gives you a feeling of power, because you know you are basically weak!' I goaded him. 'As for you, Raoul! How can you be proud to be this monster's son? I do not understand – Doctor Médoc was so gentle and good—'

'Until it came to the bit,' sneered Haabe. 'He found out about my arrival here. Raoul had secreted me in the attics, but he spotted me. Then he was too afraid to do anything about it, because of the disgrace the full story would bring on him. The cuckolded husband! He would never have held up his head again.

'From that moment he was in our hands. He had to do what we ordered. He even helped bury Jules, and it was actually his idea that I should play the part of the old hermit. He thought it safer that way, than living in the villa. That was why he was the only one who could visit me!'

'Of course! I had forgotten that.' I gritted my teeth. 'He did his best to keep me away, but he knew how stubborn I could be and how fond of Jules I was. I might have sneaked up here behind his back and discovered the true set-up!'

'Yes. You were our stumbling block. The one person we

had to fear. I realized that the instant I saw you peer at me through the window that day,' said Haabe, 'and for the moment, you made me lose my head, and I followed you down to the river and tried to shoot you. After that, however, we decided on subtler means of disposing of you. We didn't want your death to look like murder.'

'So you arranged a little landslide for my benefit,' I looked scornfully at Raoul. 'No doubt it was you who telephoned your father, or rather ex-father, from Cannes to say which car I would be travelling home in.'

'I did that well, did I not?' smirked Raoul. 'You thought I was taking Annemarie to make you jealous!'

'No,' I looked at him steadily. 'I thought, and I still do, that you were infatuated by Madame Cordet. You were not trying to make me jealous when you blurted out that you intended to marry her, and nothing could stop you. You meant what you said, and now I understand why you were so positive! With your share of the Mercredi fortune, you could well afford to keep her in her accustomed luxury.'

I glared at them. 'That is where you are both wrong. There will be no life of future luxury for you – you will never find the fortune! Never!'

'And how do you think you will stop us?' mocked Haabe. 'Tonight you will have an unfortunate accident. You will be found at the foot of the gorge, dead, of course, with a bunch of wild flowers from the cliffs still clutched in your hand!'

'No one will believe it was an accident,' I challenged them. 'You see,' I went on triumphantly, 'the police and my grandfather, and one or two others, know that the shooting incident by the war memorial was no accident! They know the boulder which narrowly missed me on the Col road was deliberately levered over the side! They know, even, that the mushrooms which killed Madame de Jarenté were meant for me! This very afternoon, Sergeant Duval is sending for extra police to make a thorough search of this area to find the person who is trying to kill me!'

'They will never dream of searching this cottage,' said Haabe, but there was uncertainty in his tone.

'Who knows you came here?' snapped Raoul suddenly.

'My grandfather will guess, and Martha. I was talking about it—'

'Your grandfather will not be home until late this evening. He told me so himself,' Raoul looked at Haabe. 'But there is now no doubt we shall have to get rid of her the moment night falls.'

He frowned. 'I shall ask my mother to help me carry her to the car from here, and we shall arrange our accident many miles from here to divert the searchers.'

I went weak with panic and my knees felt as if they would collapse under me.

These two men, ruthless father and equally ruthless son, would let nothing nor no one get in the way of their desires, and the woman, Madame Médoc, was every bit as bad. These were the three figures Monsieur Vincennes had seen searching the river bank so methodically: the three people who had rediscovered, and reburied, Jules Lamartine.

My eyes went to the little window high up on the wall. Already darkness was beginning to fall, and darkness spelled my doom.

My blood ran so cold, I was beyond shivering.

It was too late. There was no one who could save me now. The hour of my execution was at hand.

CHAPTER TWENTY-THREE

Haabe and Raoul left the bedroom and I was alone, my throbbing wrists tied so tightly to the bed post that it was agony to make the slightest move. Yet I had to move!

I was not going to stay where I was without making some effort to escape, and although all the odds seemed against me, once Raoul left the shack to go for his mother, if I freed myself I would only have Haabe to contend with.

I looked searchingly round the little room, wondering

what I could use for a weapon to overpower him, and all the time desperately trying to undo my bonds.

The bedroom was simply furnished, with its iron-framed bedstead, a box converted into a bookcase, and a rush chair. I couldn't help noticing that the crucifix which had always hung over Jules' bed had been removed, leaving an unfaded pattern. Apparently even a soulless man like Haabe could not bear to have this reminder of the Christian faith hanging over him in sorrow.

I pulled and tugged at the leather bond in growing despair, and I had almost given up all hope when a more urgent jerk than any previous one slightly eased its grip, and the leather slithered a fraction down the post. In so doing, my wrists scratched against a raw metallic edge of the bed rail.

Again, hope sparked through me. If I could keep rubbing the imprisoning thong against this knife-sharp edge, I might still have a chance to free myself!

In the living-room, I could hear Haabe pacing restlessly up and down, but he made no attempt to come near the bedroom.

I kept rubbing the back of my wrists wildly up and down the post, praying with all the prayers I knew. Sweat streamed from me. The pain in the back of my hands was pure agony since, unable to see and judge precisely what I was doing, I sometimes scraped my bare wrists and not the leather against that cutting edge.

I was almost fainting from fear and exhaustion, and had about given up the ghost, when one of the bands snapped!

I could have cried out in my excitement as I wriggled my right hand free, and with its trembling fingers, managed to unbuckle that part of the belt which secured me to the bed post.

Hastily I freed my other hand, and although I longed for a second of time to rub the pain from my wrists, even a moment was too precious to spare.

I ran softly across to the little window, opened it, and stifling a gasp as pain indescribable radiated from the torn backs of my wrists, I hauled myself up and through the narrow opening and dropped to the ground outside, where I lay crouched against the shadow of the house, listening for footsteps which might warn me of Raoul's return, and wondering if I could make a quick dash for safety.

The difficulty was, there was only one way from the shack direct to the village, the narrow track between the rocks up which I had come so gaily such a short time ago. If I did not manage to get down this track before Raoul and his mother left their house, I could be trapped once more.

Hugging the shadows, I ran lightly round to the front of the house and peered down the path, but the steep sides plunged into deep gloom, and with the moon not yet up and a low, damp mist swirling in wraith-like patches ahead of me, I could see nothing beyond a few yards.

I was steeling myself for my dash to safety, when a figure suddenly loomed from the darkness of the path and I darted once more to the side of the house, where I crouched, breathlessly.

There was a hammering on the door of the shack.

'Lucille? Are you there?' called a worried voice, and my heart hammered against my ribs as I recognized Greg's Highland lilt. At the same time, I realized that Haabe's instinctive reaction to the call would be to dash into the bedroom to keep me from crying for help – and the moment he opened the door, he would see I was missing, and then—

My mind baulked at what might happen next, but I realized there was only one thing to do.

I dashed to the front of the house, grabbed a startled Greg by the arm, and pulled him up the pathway and behind a boulder, at the very moment that Haabe, a shotgun in his hand, wrenched open the front door and stepped out.

'Greg! We have to get away from here!' I whispered the obvious. 'That is the man who has been trying to kill me!'

'But—'

'Please, Greg, this is no time for buts!' I nudged him. 'There is only one possible thing to do now. Follow me!'

Keeping the boulder between me and Haabe, I started to climb up the glacier path.

Greg came silently after me, caught my arm and said,

'Why can't we dodge past him and get to the village? We could be trapped up here!'

'We could be trapped down there!' I nodded back down the trail. 'Look!' I pointed to where two further figures had joined the German, who stood at the door of the hut, silhouetted against the light from inside.

'Rudi!' I could hear Haabe's words quite clearly, as no doubt I was meant to. 'They must be skulking quite near. You take the other shotgun and guard the path to the village. We are far enough from the first houses for you to shoot without disturbing anyone – and remember – don't hesitate. There are two of them against us now. They must both be dealt with!'

He moved back over the threshold of the house, but we could still hear him. 'Here's the other gun, then, Rudi. Your mother and I will follow and see if they have tried to escape upwards – but one thing is sure – up or down, there is no escape for them!'

'Who in the hell is Rudi?' asked Greg.

'Raoul. But it's a long story. If we get away, I'll tell you all about it.'

'But how can we possibly get away, going in this direction? The track peters out to a dead end. We're bound to be trapped, sooner or later. It's a long time until daylight, Lucille. They have all night to flush us out.'

'That's what they think!' I said grimly. 'But we have one chance, if you will just do as I say.' I touched his arm. 'Do you see that tree away up to the right, outlined against the sky?'

'Yes.'

'Well, that is where I'm trying to get to, or rather, to a spot a few yards from it.'

'If you think we could hide there indefinitely—'

'Please, Greg,' I interrupted crossly. 'For once, don't argue with me. I know what I am doing. Just trust me.'

His hand caught mine, and I tried not to wince from the pain in my wrist.

'I shall always do that, lass,' said Greg softly. 'Always!'

Something in the tone of his voice sent the blood coursing excitedly through my veins.

'And now,' he went on, almost gaily, and he grinned a devil-may-care grin which the starlight seemed to emphasize. 'Lead on, MacDuff!'

I felt a miraculous renewal of strength at his encouragement and softly touching his arm, and looking up into the face I had grown to love, I whispered,

'I'm so glad you are with me, Greg. Now I somehow feel everything will work out all right.'

He gave my hand a quick squeeze in response, and after that we were silent, concentrating on the trail before us, climbing as swiftly and quietly as possible, and making use of every bit of scrub, every patch of myrtle and rock rose, every wreath of mist, to hide us from our enemies.

Behind us, our pursuers had no need to be so careful as we were, and below their hurrying feet they sent stones slithering down the hillside, and because of our need for caution, we were aware that they were gaining on us.

They were now so close that I could hear Madame Médoc say, somewhat breathlessly,

'Are you sure they came this way, Heinrich? There isn't a sign of them ahead.'

'Where else could they be? We searched round the house: they did not pass you and Rudi on your way up, so they must have come this way. Even in daylight, it would be difficult to tackle this old stone mountainside any other way.'

'It's Madame Médoc who is with him!' exclaimed Greg softly. 'What the blazes!'

'Keep moving, Greg. The moon will soon be up. After that, we shall have very little chance.'

We were almost halfway up the mountainside by this time but now, with anxiety, and the aching pain of my wrists, and the weariness of my legs, I found it difficult to keep up the cracking pace we would have to maintain if we wanted to gain our objective.

My legs were so leaden that as I tried to make stealthily

for the refuge of a patch of scrub, I tripped over an exposed root and sent a warning shower of stones rolling down the path.

'They are right ahead of us!' cried Heinrich triumphantly. 'We have them this time!'

I tugged Greg's jacket.

'Leave the path,' I mouthed. 'We can work our way across the rock face at this part. It will be slow, but there is plenty of cover.'

If I hadn't known every inch of that mountainside so well, from my days of walking over it with Jules, we would never have dared do what we now attempted, but I had faith in my memory of the topography of the hillside and my questing fingers found the narrow ledge I was seeking, and I wriggled up to it, Greg following closely behind me.

My aching wrists were protesting at the treatment I was meting out to them, as I moved across the rock face, clinging to every possible tuft and ledge for support, but somehow I managed to keep going, and at last we were round the hump and out of sight, though not of sound, of our pursuers.

'Look, there they are!' I heard Madame Médoc shout, and I nearly fainted with panic as Haabe fired his shotgun, but they must have been misled by the movement of a mountain hare, because the shot was aimed well away from where we had disappeared. Yet this shot warned us that Haabe meant business, and if he saw us we would not escape with our lives.

At long last, only one steep hummock separated us from our objective, but now my legs were so weary I thought I would never make it.

From only yards away, round the far side of this hummock, we could hear Haabe and Madame Médoc continuing up the trail.

'The moon is rising,' whispered Greg. 'If they continue to climb ahead of us, they will see us!'

'No!' I said fiercely. We couldn't lose now! Calling on my last reserves of energy, I picked up a stone and flung it as far down the hillside as possible into a clump of shrubs.

It landed with an agreeable clatter.

'They were hiding down there after all!' yelled Haabe. 'After them! They won't escape us this time,' and he went scrambling back down the slope.

'Now!' I nudged Greg, and in a final desperate spurt I ran crouched to where the lonely tree clung precariously to the sheer mountainside.

We were now momentarily hidden from the other two by the trunk of the tree and an outcropping of volcanic rock.

I bent down, pushed my way behind a sturdy growth of yellow Genista, beckoned Greg to follow, and then whispering to him to help, I started to lift to one side a pile of miscellaneous rock and stones.

'This is the opening to a funnel of rock,' I explained hastily. 'It is the old escape route of the Resistance, known only to Jules, the Mercredis and my father, who told me about it. We must pray it hasn't been affected by landslides since these days!'

To our relief, as we tugged away the stones, a hole was revealed in the mountainside. I wriggled through and Greg followed, and then we both tried to pull back as many stones over the entrance as we could to hide it from our enemies' eyes.

'The flowering broom should be camouflage enough,' I said as I piled stones from inside the little cave across the entrance, 'but I want to be doubly sure.'

I dragged an extra large stone to the entrance, but it was so heavy it made me cry out with the pain in my wrists, and I suddenly felt I could do no more.

I sat down wearily on the rocky base of the odd funnel-like cavity, which led from this spot almost sheerly up to the top of the mountain, opening out on the side of the Alp away from the stone glacier, the side which overlooked the valley that ran parallel to the Lune.

'Thank goodness, your father told you about this!' Greg crawled to my side. 'We should have been lost otherwise.'

'Greg!' I started to sob. 'Those people killed Jules! They murdered him, the way they would have murdered me if they could.'

'Hush, my darling,' Greg put his arm round me and drew me to him, comfortingly, as he had done after our near escape on the Col.

'Greg!' I clung to him. 'I'm sorry I brought you into this mess.'

'You always seem to be getting into a mess!' he said teasingly, but tenderly.

I sniffed. 'What made you come looking for me at Jules' shack?' I wanted to know. 'If you hadn't—'

'I came, you stubborn young woman, because something about your tone when you were speaking to me on the telephone told me you were up to something! You're not a convincing distorter of the truth, Lucille! Lies don't go with your nature.'

'What do you know about my nature?' I challenged him. 'You hardly know me.'

'Don't I?' he said. 'I know you are as rash as you are stubborn, so I finished my work quickly, dashed to your house to find it empty, and guessed you had come on here.' He hugged me even tighter.

'Thank goodness, my guess was right!' he said shakily. 'But in future, my lass, you will do as you are told, do you hear?'

'I will not be ordered around like a child!' I flared.

'Darling!' he sighed. 'Must you always argue with me?'

He pulled me round, so that although it was dark and we could not see each other, I knew we were face to face.

'How about a truce, my love?'

I could hardly believe my ears. We were in darkness, but now it was as if a great light had dawned.

'Say that again!' I whispered, trembling.

'Say what?' he teased, and then once more he took me in his arms, but this time there was passion, not comfort, in his clasp, and as he bent to kiss me and as his lips met mine, we forgot our danger; forgot we had still a long, hard way ahead of us.

It wasn't the right time or the right place, but when love comes, there is never time, nor place, only eternity.

CHAPTER TWENTY-FOUR

For a long time Greg and I stood, locked in each other's arms, whispering a million stupid questions and endearments.

It was Greg who at last pulled us back to the present.

'Darling Lucille,' he said softly, 'if we want to keep our date with the preacher, the sooner we get away from here the better!'

'I suppose so,' I sighed. 'Greg! I love you so! And to think I imagined you were in love with Annemarie!'

'I was only trying to keep her away from Raoul for your sake, because I thought you were in love with him.'

'Never!' I said vehemently. 'I was never in love with him, and now I hate him! As much for being Haabe's son as for the dreadful things he has done.'

'Haabe's son!' echoed Greg. 'What on earth—'

Hastily I explained what I had learned and then, since it would have been stupid to linger longer, we worked our way slowly up the funnel.

If Greg hadn't been with me, I should never have made it. My wrists were red hot with pain and as I pulled myself foot by foot upward, I kept scraping my legs and knees and ankles against unseen edges of rock.

Often I would have slithered back if Greg had not steadied me and helped me onwards, but at last we pulled ourselves through the funnel head, out into the clear night air.

We paused for breath on the gently sloping, grassy hillside which rolled evenly down into the valley of the river which ran parallel to the Lune, and as I gazed about me from the star patterned sky to the hillside silvered with the light of the now fully risen moon, I knew how my father must have felt when he, too, had used this escape route.

An hour later, as the first rays of the sun stalked over the high Alps, we reached the hamlet in the valley and put a telephone call through to my grandfather, telling him what had happened, knowing that he would take the necessary steps to capture the infamous trio.

Four hours later, when Greg and I eventually managed to get transport back to Tourloup, it was all over.

Heinrich Haabe, Raoul and his mother had been caught and taken to prison, all three to stand trial for the murders that had been committed in their greed to possess the Mercredi fortune.

My grandfather greeted my return with tears in his eyes, and Martha wept openly as she came running down the garden path to gather me in her arms, regardless of my dusty and disreputable appearance.

Before we could relax, however, Greg and I had to go to the police station to make our statements.

We came back to the Villa Beau Site together, but Greg left me at the gate.

'I can hardly ask your grandfather for permission to marry you dressed like this!' he teased.

'Oh, Greg!' I said blissfully. 'I'm glad I didn't dream what took place at the foot of the funnel!'

'It certainly wasn't a dream,' said Greg firmly, 'and you aren't backing out of what you promised then!'

Martha, unaware of what was about to happen, came out to tell me she had laid out fresh clothes for me, and I was to hurry because luncheon would be served in half an hour.

'Could we ask Monsieur MacIntosh to join us?' I said slyly. 'He has never tasted your cooking.'

'Assurément!' she beamed at Greg. 'You will always be welcome here, Monsieur, after what you did for our Lucille!'

I winked at Greg over her shoulder and he grinned back, and then went hurrying off down the road to return, less than half an hour later, looking his handsome best in a smart dark suit and gleaming white shirt.

I was waiting at the door to meet him, and I almost danced him through the house and out on to the terrace, where Grandpère was sipping an apéritif.

'Grandpapa, Greg wants to ask you something,' I said with a blush.

Grandfather looked from one to the other of us and his smile broadened with beaming pleasure.

'I hope I have guessed the question!' he said happily. Greg nodded, and took my hand.

'You don't mind another Scotsman in the family?' he asked, as Martha's tabby cat strolled on to the terrace and rubbed herself against his ankles.

Grandpère shook his head.

'I knew you were the man for Lucille,' he said knowingly, 'so now, chérie,' he turned to me, 'let us fill our glasses and toast your happy future.'

'My future!' I said, half sadly. 'It seems heartless to feel so happy when, if it hadn't been for me, Madame de Jarenté and her companion would still be alive.'

'You must not think of that, my dear,' said Greg gently. 'Remember only that the day before she died, an old lady, who craved for death as we do for sleep, said we had given her one of the happiest days she had had.'

'And Jules . . .' I sighed.

'Jules was getting very frail,' said Grandpère. 'He would not have survived another winter, and at least he died knowing that, because of him, Haabe would never discover the coveted treasure of the Mercredis.'

'How could he be sure of that?' exclaimed Greg. 'Haabe had an idea where to look, and with German thoroughness, he would have searched every inch of the ruins.'

Grandpère looked at me, and I looked from him to the man I was going to marry; the man I knew I could trust all my days. The man who would never betray my secret.

'Haabe could never have found the Mercredi treasure, Greg, because, at the end of the war, with his weak, mutilated hands, Jules dug it all up and buried it where now only you and I and Grandpère know of: in the only place from which it will never be moved.

'The treasure of the Mercredis lies below their burial place, under the memorial to their heroism in the valley!'

There was a long silence. Then I lifted up my glass.

'To Jules and his secret!'

'And our loyalty to him!' Grandfather clinked his glass against mine.

'And to this family!' ended Greg, raising his glass to ours.

We pledged our toast, and when we had done so, we solemnly flung our empty glasses over the railing, down into the ravine.

I took the arms of the two men I loved, and together we walked across the terrace to the dining-room, where Martha was waiting to serve our lunch.

She looked at our smiling faces in surprise, and so I let go of Grandfather's arm and, taking Greg's hand in mine, I went up to her and happily, because with our toast we had dispelled the ghost of sorrow and bitterness, jealousy and fear, I told her that her dearest wish was going to come true, and that before the first snows of autumn fell on the Mountain of the Lune, she would be dancing at my wedding!